SLEEPING DRAGONS

SLEEPING DRAGONS

MAGELA BAUDOIN

TRANSLATED FROM THE SPANISH
BY WENDY BURK AND M.J. FIÈVRE

SCHAFFNER PRESS
TUCSON, ARIZONA

*For my father, because with him
I have become six years old again:
six years of glorious salvation.*

*For Sergio T., in the most
imperfect synchronicity.*

CONTENTS

POSTPONED CONFESSIONS: THE SHORT STORIES OF MAGELA BAUDOIN

THE CATEGORIZATION of literary genres is, if course, a convention imposed by academics and publishers, although we as readers know that these genres reflect an intuitive literary truth: when we read a short story, we know that we are not reading a novel. The difficulty lies in defining these conventional categories. The short story, perhaps even more so than the novel or the essay, is a mysterious genre. It is less grandiloquent than the novel and less formal than the essay. As the distillation of a single episode, with a concentrated focus on one event or one character, it suggests the aristocratic hierarchy of an anecdote or joke. It is short—yes—but it aims at portraying or containing an entire world.

Magela Baudoin's short stories are certainly unique. While meticulously observed, they speak of secrets and allude to something ever greater than the argument they propose. Although Baudoin seems to tell us her stories with the most apparent frankness, we readers sense behind her words a dark reticence, unconfessed motives and secret reasons, people and places whose names Baudoin would rather not remember. The explicit, frank, open appearance of her stories deceives us, but with such skill that we agree to be deceived. The atmospheres she creates are threatening, gloomy, stormy. There are hints of humor, but her smile is sardonic, full of irony, accusing. We come to the last page of a Baudoin story and we ask ourselves, *what exactly just happened*? What is the real story behind this story? We understand the intricacies of the plot, from beginning to end, the setting, the voices of the men and women who populate Baudoin's pages, and yet something essential seems to escape us. What is it that we did not grasp, what is it that should not have been lost on us?

Borges, the master of the short story (although in a notably different register) observed that perhaps the aesthetic fact is "the imminence of a revelation that does not take place." This quality of postponed promise defines the delicate narratives of Magela Baudoin.

ALBERTO MANGUEL
CHRISTMAS 2015
NEW YORK

SLEEPING DRAGONS

SOMETHING FOR DINNER

For Facundo

WHEN IT WAS ALL OVER, Mom made us promise we would never bring up the subject again. And we didn't. She raised us to never tell lies. I guess all mothers do that. But for her, "to never tell lies" meant—and this was something I could only convince my brother of after many years had gone by—not only to always speak the truth, but also something much more basic. She believed it was wrong to lie to others, but even worse to lie to yourself. What Mom hated most of all was lying to save your own skin, or to take the easy way out, or to make yourself look good. How can I put it? She thought you were better off burning in hell honestly than lying your way into purgatory.

More than once we saw her blanch with shame—because sincerity can be inhibiting—and still bring herself to tell the truth. Mom was a nurse; and when I say that, what I mean is she was cold as ice. She was constantly working, usually at night in people's homes, which paid better but still didn't pay enough in the end, and was less stable. Days she worked in a public hospital, where the salaries were strictly national but the general tone was presumptuously foreign. This didn't bother Mom as much as it did her fellow nurses. At least she had a job, she liked to remind us; we had a lot to be thankful for. In saying this, she was really trying to convince my brother, whose favorite sport as an adolescent was contradicting her, and who hated the annual holiday party, to which the entire staff of the hospital—doctors, nurses, administrators, social workers, lawyers, and even the custodian—brought their kids.

Mom always took us to the party, even though six kids made a lot of noise. In general, six kids were a challenge to feed and keep in line. That's why no one ever invited us over their house, and why she kept our doors open to everyone. No matter how many extra kids showed up at our house for dinner, she always managed, as if by magic, to feed us all. Anyway, we never missed her office Christmas party—first because there was a ton of food, second because it was usually a picnic, and third and best because they gave out presents. Our poor mother. Presents rained down from the heavens on her, like some kind of sad little holiday bonus. As for us kids, I won't lie, we always got a kick out of trying to mix oil and water by hanging out with the doctors' kids at the party.

My brother loved to embarrass Mom, to test her. It was his way of saying, "Let's see you try to play the martyr this time!" Not infrequently, he told me, or rather confessed to me, he was bad without even trying. But one consequence of Mom's complete honesty was that she was also completely predictable. When it came to raising us, she didn't go by theory and she didn't believe in dialogue. She never stopped us from saying anything, even if it was something we might regret. She spanked you twice and was done with it, or she threw whatever was within arm's reach: her hairbrush, the wooden spoon, the rolling pin, a saucepan, a couple of oranges from the fruit basket....But usually she whipped off her slipper and hit you on the back of the thighs, two whacks. It really didn't hurt much—at least that's what I remember—because with Mom, the punishment was more about the shouting than anything else. Also because, deep down inside, each one of us kids knew that we deserved it, which softened the blow.

Mom wasn't the type to hold a grudge, unlike my brother, who was the only boy in the house. We girls got over our anger soon enough, but he stayed mad and yelled at her, "I hate you!" He said it over and over, to hurt her, because he was the one who got spanked the most. Which, by the way, gradually stopped seeming unfair to us, and became just another fact of life. I know it's not possible that he was the guilty party for every single infraction that occurred when we were growing up. But the truth is that Mom eventually stopped asking us who did it, because the answer she received was always the same. So often enough, she saved her breath and just reached for the wooden spoon.

My brother, like my mom, was cold as ice. And like her, it took a lot to make him melt. He almost never cried, not even when she died. In fact, when I was a child, I only remember him crying once. You see, he didn't mind getting spanked if he had a chance to get even. And, at one of the hospital Christmas parties, he did. He told some of the doctors' kids that Mom hit us. He didn't give a lot of details but he was clear on the concept: "Yeah," he said, indicating the backs of his thighs, "my mom hits us." The other boys laughed, and my brother became emphatic.

"If you don't believe me," he dared them, "why don't you go and ask her!"

The boys exchanged glances, smiling maliciously. Evil can

be infinitely pure when you're eleven. My brother showed no mercy. He watched them run over to the cluster of adults where Mom stood in conversation, surrounded by doctors, administrators, all the important people from the hospital.

"Ma'am," they shouted, laughing, "is it true that you hit your son?" The adults were shocked into silence. Mom went red as a beet, and even from a distance we saw her vacillate, but not for long.

"Sure," she told them with self-conscious dignity, "when he asks for it, he gets his spanking." All the adults laughed.

When we got home, we girls thought that he was in for at least ten whacks with the slipper, but all she said was, "Well, there you have it, revenge is a dish best served cold, eh?" She didn't look angry or upset. Her emotion only showed in her eyes and in her lips, which trembled ever so slightly. And even though he didn't get punished, my brother cried all night long, very quietly, as if she'd beaten him black and blue. I heard him, from the top of the bunk bed. All five of us sisters listened to him cry.

That wasn't the first or the last trick played by my brother. Mom bore with his pranks and later retold the stories with gusto, a bit proud of his audacity. Only a mother can extract tenderness from her children's misdeeds. Looking back now, I believe that her old-school way of raising us paved the way for my brother's infamous reputation, which came to precede him. In fact, it became a point of honor for him to confirm it.

She never kept a husband for long. I think she ended up enjoying the heroism of being a single mom: just her and her kids, against the world. But the truth—the gospel truth, as my brother liked to say—was that Mom was also afraid of being alone. She derived strength and support from the compassion she received from others. Everyone admired her because, in addition to her six children, she always had a lazy slacker at home to take care of. Five husbands in succession, during the years we were all in the house. "Father" was a useless word in our childhood. My brother used it for the first time when he turned seven. All of a sudden he got downcast, moody, didn't want to eat.

"What's wrong with you today?" Mom asked. She touched her lips to his forehead to see if he had a temperature.

"Nothing," he answered, looking down at the floor.

"Nothing? Then why are you so quiet?"

"I miss Daddy."

She hesitated, looked at him with guilt in her eyes, and went and brought him some Jell-O.

As far as I'm concerned, if he had pulled that number once or twice and left it there, none of us would have ever been the wiser. But he always carried things too far. And one day Mom, who was by no means slow on the uptake, really let him have it.

"Liar!" she yelled. "You don't even remember your father!"

"Of course I do."

"Well then, it's about time you forgot him."

My brother just went on playing with his toy car, as if she hadn't spoken. Mom could be colder than an ice chest.

"You listen to me." She grabbed him by the collar. "Your father might have loved you, but he left. I'm the one who feeds you and clothes you. So I'm your mother and I'm your father, and that's it. Understand?"

"Yeah," he said, a wide grin splitting his face, "I know," and he was off running.

Mom hated lies so much that she once put fresh chile peppers in my brother's mouth to teach him not to tell people that she was a doctor, instead of a nurse. His teacher ran into Mom at the hospital and then asked him in front of the whole class if she worked there. All the other students went silent. My brother swallowed hard, like he always did when he knew he was about to tell a lie.

"Yes, miss," he said, nodding. "My mom's a doctor."

The teacher made a fuss over him, her praises salted with more than a little self-interest, while the other students gritted their teeth with envy and my brother began to get a sinking feeling in his chest. "It was like a dagger," he told me. A few days later, when the teacher asked Mom for a physical exam, she almost keeled over with rage.

"The next time you tell a lie, you're getting the seeds," she shouted, while my brother crunched on the chile peppers without shedding a single tear.

When he turned thirteen, my brother learned how to drive. I can't remember who taught him, but he already knew how to warm up Mom's old Renault. He loved driving it forward a couple of feet and then backing it up. He'd agree to go shopping with her because then she would let him get the car from the garage and bring it around to the front of the house.

"When I really know how to drive," my brother promised, taking her by the arm, "I'll bring you to see your patients at night and I'll wait for you in the car until you're finished."

My mother gave him a half smile lit by her own peculiar blend of pessimism and wary faith.

"Wanna make a bet?" he shot back. "Let me have the car and you'll see, no one will drive better than me!"

"We'll see about that."

But "we'll see about that" wasn't the same as "never bring up the subject again." As far as my brother was concerned, my mother's response held an implicit promise, a reality that was as proximate as he was stubborn. Learning to drive became his only interest in life. He spent hours practicing on the living room couch, shifting an imaginary gear stick. He talked endlessly about four- and six-cylinder engines, about Formula One champion drivers—Fangio, Ascari, Farina, Niki Lauda, Emerson Fittipaldi, Ayrton Senna, Schumacher, etc.—and about the virtues of manual versus automatic transmission. Mom's car was a stick shift, and he was a little bit in love with it.

"Mom, everyone knows that driving stick is the best!" he told her. She just laughed.

Marlon and Josué, my brother's friends, followed his lead. He instilled in them his passion for driving, along with his recklessness. Josué was the son of a horse trainer from Brazil. His family struggled to stay afloat, like ours did. No, even more so. Sometimes Josué walked into our kitchen starving and devoured whatever lay in his path like a swarm of giant ants. His dad didn't have a car; he was a nice man, always willing to help out. Mom liked him. Marlon's stepfather, on the other hand, was really something special: at least that's what Mom said, under her breath, because she did her best not to speak ill of anybody. She wouldn't allow us to repeat what the whole neighborhood said about him, because we didn't have any proof. What I can say for certain is that Marlon's stepfather had a Chrysler LeBaron with a manual transmission and tinted windows, which he said was a taxi, but which no one ever saw him use as such, and that he always had cash on hand. He spent his days cruising in the car, always with the same group of people, and he spent his nights out on the street, drinking. He hit Marlon and his mother, not with a slipper but in a way that was impossible to describe. Mom had treated them once at the hospital. Like Josué, Marlon was always starving. He also devoured whatever lay in his path, but after he'd already eaten at home. His stepfather told him, "Go on and get it." And Marlon came to our house and got it. Mom didn't mind.

"If he's here, it's because he needs it," she told us, "and he's welcome to it."

One day at our house for dinner, right after he'd finished washing the LeBaron, Marlon told us, "It's a waste to have a car and not use it."

My brother's eyes began to gleam.

"Forget about the car and come eat," Mom said. She stole pitying glances at Marlon when he wasn't looking. Marlon's face always looked closed down somehow, even when he laughed.

That car became an obsession for all three of them. It started with their washing the LeBaron as many afternoons as possible. That meant any afternoon when Marlon's stepdad slept in instead of going out and cruising. My mom didn't like to see her son do someone else's bidding, but in truth he did it because he wanted to. They all did. They popped the hood, checked the oil, brakes, and exhaust, and even inspected the hidden mechanisms inside the doors. They spent hours sitting on the curb, not even touching the car, just studying it, guided by the intuition of my brother and Marlon, who had worked together as helpers in an auto shop during school vacation. My brother would try to boost Marlon's confidence by repeating some of Mom's encouraging clichés, and Marlon would nod silently. Before long, the LeBaron was the cleanest car on the block.

"What do I have to do to get you to wash my car like that?" Mom chided.

"Pay us," said my brother, in his best macho voice.

"Pay you? How much?"

"A ton."

"Oh yeah?" Mom said, "then forget about it."

We girls knew he was lying. And Mom wasn't fooled either. Marlon's stepdad never gave them so much as a "thank you." In fact, he was the kind of guy who would charge them for the privilege of touching his car. He dogged Marlon and humiliated him, especially in front of his friends. "Hurry up!" he yelled as Marlon washed the exterior. "Hurry it up, dumbass." Marlon washed faster. "Hurry the fuck up, imbecil!" he taunted. "He's useless, just like his mother." Marlon dreamed of killing him. One time, with my brother and Josué as witnesses, the man dug a pair of panties out of the backseat, sniffed them, and shoved them in Marlon's face before tucking them away in his pocket. "Don't you go taking stuff out of my car, you got that?" he growled. My brother and Josué did their best to look away, while Marlon bit back his anger, because the only thing that mattered was learning how to drive, and the LeBaron was their ticket.

My brother's mission in life, then, was to teach them to drive; and their mission was to make sure nobody found out what they were doing. They planned it well, limiting themselves to brief excursions, fraught with nerves and adrenaline. On the day of the disaster, my brother turned the key in the ignition. The car lunged forward asthmatically because he'd forgotten to put it in neutral. He realized his mistake and turned off the motor, then took a few deep breaths to calm down. "Stupid," he said out loud. He shifted into neutral before turning the key again. This time it worked. He shifted into first and took off slowly, driving forward about ten feet. Then he backed up, leaving the car right where it started. His friends followed suit. Josué went next; he was more of a natural driver. Marlon, alas, was not. The car groaned when he took the wheel because he struggled with keeping the clutch down while shifting into first.

"Come on, let's do this," my brother said, summoning all

of his force of personality. Marlon eased into the driver's seat while the other boys encouraged him.

Marlon knew he just had to go for it. "Okay… now!" he muttered as he successfully shifted into first, his knees trembling.

"Take it easy," Josué laughed, "your leg looks like it's gonna fall off!"

The street was practically deserted, like the streets always were in the middle of the afternoon. The sun beat down on the boys as intensely as if they were widows wearing mourning. Marlon's T-shirt was wet at the armpits and around his chest. His forehead shone with sweat. "It's time, we're ready," he said, in a steely voice. Josué and my brother shot each other a look. "Let's do this"—Marlon raised his voice, resolute—"or are you gonna wuss out?"

The street behind ours led to a grammar school and a police station, so traffic swelled during the rush hours, especially at dismissal, when it teemed with children and parking cars. Marlon decided to seize the moment and let loose.

"Who's scared?" he yelled, slapping the steering wheel with the palm of his hand.

His words were met with silence. For a moment he saw himself utterly abandoned.

"Who's scared, dickheads?" growled my brother, coming to Marlon's rescue.

"Nobody!" the three of them shouted.

My brother felt a little worried, in spite of how often they'd discussed this moment, but the idea of the open road called to him. It was the destiny they had dreamed of. After a flawless start, he pulled smoothly away from the curb, waving at our neighbor Micaela who was working in her store. She was my mother's friend, so he knew Mom was going to find out sooner or later. He shifted into first gear and even switched into second, at exactly the moment when the acceleration made the transmission start to shake. He had made it practically all the way around the block when he slowed down to let a van pass, turned right, entered our side street, and braked abruptly at the curb. His legs were trembling too, he confessed to me later.

Next up was Josué, who had never aspired to be the smartest, the best, or the most macho. "I'm nervous," he blurted out. No one responded.

Josué didn't get the LeBaron started smoothly, but he did get it started, and he drove it around the block as sedately as if it were a horse-drawn carriage, without even needing to shift gears. When he made it past the grammar school, the street was already full of parked cars, but there were no kids in sight. My brother took a deep breath. Josué continued his journey around the block with infinite slowness, then stopped the car and jumped out as fast as if he'd been ejected.

"My hands are all sweaty," he said, drying them on his jeans. My brother looked at his face and burst out laughing. To tell the truth, it was nervous laughter.

Marlon was next. He didn't look excited and confident anymore. My brother said he was green, as if he were about to puke.

"We can stop now, if you want," my brother told him.

But Marlon didn't hesitate. He changed places with Josué. He didn't take any deep breaths; he didn't shift into neutral; he didn't do any of the things they had carefully practiced. He didn't even cross himself like the three of them always did before starting the car. He just yanked on the key. The car lunged forward but then got started. Marlon accelerated and prepared to shift gears. He even put on his blinker to turn right. He had that same look in his eye, my brother told me afterwards, that provoked so much pity in our mom.

"Slow down, man!" Josué yelled. "You're gonna get us all killed."

Instead of slowing down, Marlon floored it as he went into the turn. The car roared and reared, barely missing a bus, a motorcycle, a taxi, and even a horsecart. Then, from out of nowhere, a woman appeared, stopped dead in the middle of the road, holding two kids by the hand. It was too late to slam on the brakes. My brother jerked the steering wheel hard to the right. Josué gripped the front seat and Marlon gripped the dashboard. The front end of the LeBaron crashed into the front wall of the police station. Bricks from the wall rained down on top of the smoking hood, which was crumpled up like a ball of paper.

Marlon turned around to make sure that my brother and Josué were still alive. His eyes looked like they were about to fall out of their sockets. His mouth flopped open but no words came out. My brother pushed him out of the car and then leaped out himself. "This is it, you're not going to wuss out now," he told him. Josué was the most composed of the three.

"Calm down," he said, "the cops are coming." Just then the dismissal bell rang. In an instant they found themselves surrounded by shouting adults and screaming children. In my brother's field of vision, all that existed were Josué's gestures, the seats of the car exposed to view by the open doors, and the big wet spot on Marlon's jeans: all that remained of his fear and, also, his courage. The police asked who was driving at the time of the accident. Marlon still couldn't speak. My brother responded rapidly and mechanically, the same way he did when Mom interrogated him at home.

"Me." His voice shook and he swallowed hard.

When the police brought the boys inside the station, they

flooded them with questions, which all three of them answered without hesitation, as if they'd never learned on TV that they had the right to remain silent. They rapidly confessed who the car belonged to. The officer in charge wrote down "property of stepfather," after Marlon spelled out his full name. Then they admitted that they had each driven around the block, and the officer said out loud, "without authorization." My brother repeated that he was the one who was driving when they crashed, and that they'd never taken the car out before. The officer took this down and added "without human injury."

The police announced their intention to confiscate the car. This news filled Marlon with desperation. "Shit, shit, he's going to kill me," he said over and over, scrubbing his face with his hands and begging them not to take anything out of the car. "Why not, what's in there that's so important?" the officer asked. Josué hissed at Marlon, "Calm down, he can't do anything to you while you're in here." But Marlon just sobbed inconsolably, "You don't know what he's like, he's going to kill me!" The officer wrote this down in his little book. That's when my brother lost his temper and told Marlon, "So die already and quit crying, you dick."

The neighborhood was in such an uproar that Mom and I, driving back from the hospital in the Renault, never made it to our house. Everyone was talking about it. Micaela waved frantically at my mom and we stopped in front of her store. As my brother had anticipated, she spilled the beans right away, providing an abundance of detail. Mom drove fast to the police station. "Holy God, Holy God," she said over and over. I felt as if I had swallowed a stone.

When we got to the police station, Mom asked for the officer on duty and heard him out with exquisite patience. "Are you sure my son was driving?" she asked, because that's not what everyone in the neighborhood was saying. He explained that my brother himself had admitted it. Mom always knew how to act when things were starting to get ugly. The officer told her that, thanks to the boys' statements, he would be able to write his report quickly. Their parents could take them home after filing some paperwork and paying up. Josué's father was off somewhere in the countryside with his horses, and Marlon's stepdad was nowhere to be found. Politely, confidently, Mom told the officer that if she had to pay in order to take her son home, she would, but that she wanted to speak with him first. They let us go in while they finished inspecting the car. When we got to the cell, we saw Josué first; he was still on his feet and even waved hello to us. Marlon was huddled up in the corner with his head on his knees, while my brother was draped against the side wall of the cell. He swallowed hard when he saw us, and came forward. Mom grabbed his hands.

"Jesus Christ, son, why did you say it was you?" she asked him, very quietly, pinching his arm hard. My brother didn't try to pull away. He seemed to be searching for words.

"Mom, please, let's drop it," he begged, looking across the cell at Marlon. She followed his gaze. Marlon's eyelids were terribly swollen.

"Just wait until we get home, this time you're going to get red hot chiles." My brother's eyes started to water. Mom squeezed his hand, then said, letting her voice carry into the interior of the cell, "And how about you boys? Are you hungry? Can I bring you something for dinner?"

Back at the front desk, the officer explained to us that there was a complication: their search of the car had revealed contraband. "This is the work of a professional," he said. My brain began to fill up with images, like an old movie reel projecting scenes on the ceiling of our room at night. The police started searching for Marlon's stepdad while Mom called the lawyer who worked at the hospital. Everything else really did unfold just like in a movie. Marlon's mother dried her eyes and admitted what everyone else in the neighborhood already knew. Josué's mom was as composed as he was. As for Marlon's stepdad, it was like the earth opened and swallowed him up. They never found him, not that day, and not ever. Mom paid for the lawyer and the property damages with a loan from the hospital. Josué's parents promised to pay their share, but before too long their family went back to Brazil. Marlon's mother also left town, but that was because of my mom's advice. And my brother escaped both the slipper and the chile peppers, but that's a story we never talk about. Mom made us promise never to bring it up again, and when she died, so much time had gone by that we could barely remember.

A BUENOS AIRES
SUMMER SONATA

ELENE TOOK CARE OF everything, as usual. She found two old ladies to rent me a room while I'm in Buenos Aires, enrolled in the class we had both wanted to take. Such are the hideous courtesies you derive from being at death's door: she gave up her place to me when we realized we couldn't afford the tuition for two. One more reason for me to be in her debt. At this point, I don't know how much more I could possibly be in anyone's debt. I'll make a list, to spare her the trouble of making it for me, so at least I won't be in her debt for that too. First, she left everything behind to move in with me. In her case, this was quite a feat, because it was her family, not mine, who were the inquisitors, ready to skin her alive in a cauldron of boiling oil. For me it was easy: I was older. My parents were hippies, and I suspect that they felt a secret satisfaction at being able to show off their 'different' daughter. Besides, being ten years older was always an advantage until now; it's only recently that it's become a bill to be settled, a divine retribution, a defeat of the flesh.

Second, she left everything behind to let me be the one to shine: the fellowship, the foreign correspondent gig, the travel, with Elene trailing behind me. She left behind her studies at the conservatory to follow me and, although I never asked her to, no one remembers that anymore, not least of all because Elene is so considerate that she changes the subject if someone recalls with nostalgia what a great violinist she was and what might have been, if only... Third, she left everything behind, yet again, to save me from dying of fear while I went through chemo. It's not a romantic exaggeration: Elene has done it all for me. And that fact, which never gave me anything except control, is destroying me now because I'm the one who needs her, and I can't bear it.

This was supposed to be a breather for us, but Elene won't stop calling... She's in hysterics about the cockroaches. That's what I get for being an idiot: what business do I have trying to be funny? I had to hang up because I was about to kill her. The old ladies have therapeutic names: Remedios and Milagros— Remedies and Miracles.

After lunch Remedios and Milagros got into an argument. Reme yelled and Mili refused to acknowledge her, until Remedios yelled louder, to back her into a corner, to control her, and only then did Mili answer, "Yes, Reme, I heard you!" It reminded me of my own fights with Elene, and I'm not going to say who was who. Poor things; they didn't sell anything today. On top of that, the water heater broke. I went on washing the dishes as imperceptibly as I could, but as I was putting away the big griddle, I turned too fast and collided with the kitchen cabinet. The sharp end of the shelf rammed into my forehead—

or, rather, my forehead slammed into the sharp end of the shelf—with the pithy violence of a hammer blow. Griddle on the floor; both women turning their focus to me. That's how it is when you're a guest. The two of them are exaggeratedly attentive.

My accident proved to be Mili's salvation as she slipped away with her bags. Reme, on the other hand, vented the remainder of her fury on me. "What on earth have you done?" she said, obviously still stewing about the cold water, while I clutched my head, "Don't worry, it's nothing." I thought that this would be the perfect moment for a cockroach to appear and distract us both with the task of chasing and killing it. She would have emptied the bottle of roach killer over the bug, the countertop, the whole kitchen, all the while trying to convince me that it's not because their house isn't clean. But we both know the truth. That's why, as soon as they go out for the day, I clean everything. I do it like a sprinter, bleaching every surface in the apartment, which thankfully is as tiny as a comma. I try not to linger in the kitchen, even though I know it's the room that needs it most. But I can't. It sickens me. The two of them know what I do while they're out, but they don't say a word. Why try to justify poverty? "It's the summertime," they explained to me today. In this heat, who wants shoelaces? Sometimes I pray for rain, just so that people will take off their sandals and wear shoes for a change. The problem is that it gets even hotter after it rains. I've never understood the law of large numbers, why it is that in a city as immense as Buenos Aires, they're able to sell so little. The two of them swear it's because the summer has been so hot, and because more people than usual have left the city. I want to believe this, but the state of their apartment suggests that their troubles have gone on for more than one summer. The walls are black with smoke, the floor is stained, the kitchen is a wreck, and you can see the yellow foam peeking out of the couch. It's white. Or, it was white, because yesterday I bought a slipcover and put it on. Reme thanked me, just like a little girl. Milagros, for once, said something different: "Honey, is that how you see us?"

If Elene had been with me, she would have reacted with the sideways frown, so unique to her, that used to make me feel ashamed for a few moments and that now, after so many years of our heroic partnership, isn't even meant as a reproach, but only a sign of weary distaste. The weary distaste produced by things that will never change, and that it's therefore useless to correct.

I'm not sure if I should write about this, especially since I'm here for such a short time. Only twelve weeks. I've already been accused once of being an unreliable narrator, and of course Elene had to be there to remind me of it. I've never apologized for being a journalist, although sometimes maybe I should have; but since it's not possible to just wander around writing down everything I see here, maybe I should convince myself that I'm making it up. That way I'll be able to tell the story without guilt. After all, that's why I came here: to pack away the tape recorder and 'write' without being in a straitjacket, even if the literature class is little more than an alibi. Maybe it would be better to convince myself of the truth: I came here to 'finish' healing, as Elene says. But can you really be healed without first breaking down?

I, who know what happiness is and who have always been a little sad for no reason, have promised myself (have promised her) to experience a 'reawakening.' It's not every day that you survive cancer as well as the tender care of the one who loves you. That's why I sit down every morning, at exactly the same time of day, to write. That's how I convince myself that I'm not double-crossing her, that this summer is something more than an act of narcissism, that it's a way for me to break free without jumping into the void. I left behind my job and a good salary. I left behind the perfect woman (so perfect she's strangling me). I left behind all of my lukewarm comforts. I reconsider this last idea and decide it would be better to write, "I left behind all the comforts of boredom." Yes, that's why I came here, and even if I don't achieve my goal, maybe this time around it'll be the therapy that cures me of all my obsessions and neuroses, because at this point I could write a whole dissertation on phobias. But how can you forget something if you haven't given it a name first?

At times I feel miserable, absolutely miserable. Today I cooked up some pasta with basil-walnut pesto and mushrooms. Mili, who never eats, and who especially never eats lunch, ate some of this. She kept on stealing glances at the price sticker on the package of walnuts. I think maybe she felt guilty about not eating, maybe she said to herself, "Who knows when I'll ever be able to eat something like this again?" The worst of it was that, right when I was starting to gloat a bit, out crawled the cockroaches. Some of them in the colander, some of them wobbling on the cups hanging from the wall, three more peeking out of the drain. Their size was between small and tiny. Reme tried to keep me from screaming; she took the utensils out of my hands while I attempted to wipe the expression off my face. Thinking about Elene, I poured roach killer down the drain. Of course, that was the end of the nice basil smell. Such admirable fucking restraint! Goddamn you, Elene.

Reme left a note taped to the fridge: *Martín will stop by today.* Her handwriting is vigorous and optimistic, just like her speech. Remedios can talk for hours on end while you offer up monosyllables, without her ever realizing. At the very bottom of the note she had written, as if she remembered it just before leaving the house, *Elene says call her.* Martín never stopped by to fix the water heater.

After class, I went to the store by the apartment building. It's Chinese-owned. Inside, there's a stand-alone fruits and vegetables section, or at least it seems to work that way, because if you buy some onions you have to pay for them there, instead of at the cash register. I couldn't help noticing the woman who works in that section. She's Bolivian, like me, I knew it at once. I maneuvered myself next to her and was stupid enough to ask, in front of everyone, where she was from. If she could have, she would have spit on me: "From Peru," she lied.

When I reached the apartment, Reme was holding supper for me. She didn't sell anything again today; she's the one who pays the bills. She traveled a long way to three different stores, Chinese-owned, but none of the owners were there. As it happened, they were all back in China. Reme was furious: "Look at the money they're making while we're killing ourselves just for a few cents." I didn't know what to say to her. I thought about words like 'Chinese mafiosos,' 'Chinese pigs,' 'Chinese capitalists,' but nothing came out. I tried to calm her down and told her about the Bolivian girl with the onions, but that was a bad idea. She got worse. She told me about how a little while ago she had to go to the hospital, because Remedios is seventy years old and she's ill. Ahead of her in line were twenty people from the slums, all Bolivians. Enraged, she cut the line in front of everyone, threatening the nurse. "You're taking me first, understand? Because this is my country!"

I remembered something by a British writer I'd recently read. He said that the history of Buenos Aires is written in the telephone book, in surnames like Romanov, Rommel, Rose, Radziwill, and Rothschild. Although Remedios doesn't want to hear it, soon it will also be written in Bolivian names like Condori, Mamani, Huanca, Parisaka, Apaza, and in Chinese names like Wang, Fung, Bai, Zhao, Yang, and Wu. Milagros keeps quiet. When you get to be their age, change isn't easy.

Today I was in a lot of pain. I called Elene and immediately regretted it. I'm done with being the incarnation of ego, the monster. Done with it. I screamed at her again that I'm not sick anymore, that she needs to leave me alone. I don't need a martyr by my side. "You know what?" I told her, "I think I'm going to stay here." She didn't answer. She cried and cried. Same old story. But this time I won't say I'm sorry.

It's Friday, the end of my first month here. Today I didn't have class and didn't feel like writing. I was a little lonely, but Reme's words rang in my head: "Who could ever get bored in this city?" Or maybe what she actually said was, "Only a moron could get bored here." The best thing to do is go for a walk, I told myself, get my fill of balconies and cornices, trees and bookstores, people on roller skates, people on bikes, buses, newsstands, flower stalls, dogs. Dogs: Labradors, Dalmatians, cocker spaniels, German shepherds, mastiffs, Samoyeds, dachshunds, poodles... Dog owners with their dogs, dog trainers with dogs, dog walkers walking dozens of dogs. Dogs with all of their consequences, and the pedestrians awkwardly attempting to sidestep those consequences. There I was in the land of consequences. I stepped in dog shit. And there's no hot water in the house.

Friday again. A good week, good stories. I got home around six. Mili was in front of the computer, like always, with her headphones on and the lights turned out. I tapped her on the shoulder. I didn't want to stay in, but I also didn't want to go to the movies alone. I asked her, she said no, I begged her. Finally she said yes. We walked twenty blocks downtown to the movie theater in Recoleta. I had already counted every block and was racking my brain about what to say to her on the way. I couldn't think of anything to talk about except the summer heat, but she could. "My favorite decade in film is the 1950s," she offered up. Me, feeling superior: "Oh, is that right?" *Stop,* I admonished myself. Mili goes out every morning to sell her wares and doesn't come home until the evening, keeping her mouth closed about what she does all day. All I know is that she doesn't sell much; Remedios told me. But now she's talking as though somebody turned on the faucet. She used to go to the movies in her hometown, Carmen de Areco, three times a week when she was a girl. I think she was in love with Gregory Peck, because she dedicated three whole blocks to him. I couldn't remember what he looked like until she told me, "He's the one in that movie about Rome with Audrey Hepburn, remember? She plays Princess Ann who goes incognito." My jaw dropped. "Did you know that was Audrey's very first leading role?" Oops: I still couldn't picture Gregory Peck. I tried to think of another actor from the same decade, to pique her: "I never liked Gregory Peck as much as Humphrey Bogart, when I saw *Casablanca* I fell in love with his voice," I said nostalgically. But she corrected me: "*Casablanca* is from the 40s, not the 50s." Oops again. "But he had a film from the 50s you must have seen," she expounded matter-of-factly, "*The African Queen*, where he starred with Katharine Hepburn. She was never as beautiful as Audrey." Oops for the third time. I thought about Elene's deathless words of wisdom: "Darling, silence is golden and speech is silver." I kept quiet while Mili talked on and on about Hitchcock's *Rear Window*, about Marlon Brando and

Vivien Leigh in *A Streetcar Named Desire*. I could only remember Vivien Leigh as Scarlett O'Hara in *Gone with the Wind*, but she mentioned at least six other movies she acted in after that one. We were almost at the movie theater, just about passing the cemetery, when she brought up Kurosawa. "*The Seven Samurai*, remember?" That one I had actually seen, but I hated it. It was my turn to make a reference, to contribute something, but it was getting late. So when we stopped in front of the posters all lit up, I let her choose the movie.

Needles in my head again. Stayed in bed all day long.

It's Friday. I only have two weeks left and I don't want to go home. I haven't called Elene. Remedios opened a bottle of Chardonnay that she got for Christmas. She's been saving it to drink with Soledad, who came over to make pizza for dinner. Sole herself brought a bottle of red, so we drank them both. Reme was happy because Martín finally came to fix the water heater, having just returned from a trip to Patagonia. Martín is a little bit slimy, in my opinion, but he is friendly: "Hey Reme, you doing all right? You're not looking so good, you know that?" This time he charged them more than 500 pesos. Hey man, at that price how could she be doing all right? I didn't even want to ask how much a new water heater would cost, but Reme was happy and that was enough. She took a hot bath after two months of compulsory cryotherapy. Then we all pitched in with dinner. Sole showed me how to make the pizza dough and called me "Miss" right up until the exact moment when we finished the first bottle. While we kneaded the dough she told me, "God knows that wine is all I have left in this world."

I sliced the pizza and Sole filled the glasses. "All right," Remedios said, and then, looking at Sole, "Well, what do you think?" Sole raised her chilled wineglass. "Pale yellow," she said, "with steely green highlights." I found the ceremony enchanting. Reme smiled and Mili held the liquid up to the light. Then Sole sniffed the wine once, swirled her glass forcefully, and sniffed it again. She was ready to make her pronouncement. "Cinnamon, pineapple, with a light but definitive aroma of vanilla." We stuck our noses in our glasses, searching out the cinnamon, while Sole took a tiny sip, swished it in her mouth for a few seconds, and swallowed. "It's fresh and brightly aristocratic, with notes of white fruits." "White fruits?" asked Reme. "Peach and coconut," she answered. We applauded. I whistled in a way that's unseemly for the dinner table, and Mili ate three bites. We toasted to Sole, the chef. Then I asked her where she had learned about food and wine, and she said on a ship or in port, she couldn't remember. Reme explained that Sole was the first Argentinian nurse to work on merchant vessels; she had traveled the globe aboard ship. "Until I lost it all," Sole added. The pizza was crisp and delicious. The bottle of wine was almost gone. Mili laughed, looking rosier than usual. "That's the beautiful thing about wine," Sole told her, refilling her glass, while I helped Reme serve the last pizza: "Times are too hard to throw away good food," she pronounced.

The second bottle of wine was a Pinot Noir, but this time Sole ceded her place to Reme, who, taking her time, described it as "deep cherry red, with ruby notes." Sole agreed. "It's elegant, with an aroma of fresh fruits and spice." Mili was the only serious one. "It seems light and fresh, but it actually has a subtle intensity, like one of those gals who just turn up in your life, stick around, and end up doing you a world of good," she said, looking at Sole and winking at me. I thought about Elene. We all applauded, except Mili, who got up to wash her plate. We toasted again, this time to Reme. "You know, honey," Sole confessed to me, having dropped the "Miss" by now, "I lost everything, I was in a psychiatric ward, I was starving, I was living on the streets, and the only one who gave me something to eat, the only one who took me in, was this woman right here." Remedios wouldn't let her finish. She barked an order, "Come on, Soledad! It's time to wash up." I cleared the table, completely drunk.

Saturday, the morning after the ball. The water heater broke again. We went back to our cryotherapy, and Reme wasn't happy about it. Milagros fled the house with her bags, and as for Martín... Martín fucked us over. It was a good idea for me to go to the library. I finally managed to finish my story from this week. My head hurt all day. It's what they call a hangover, I hope.

Friday. Elene with her violin, like the flight of the bumblebee in my head. She hasn't called, she hasn't written. After dinner, I helped the ladies sort the shoelaces and put them in boxes. They're mostly black, white, and brown; pink, green, turquoise, and yellow don't sell too well. They are beautifully simple and solid, long ones and short ones, thick and thin, cotton and synthetic. Almost nondescript. Reme and Mili walk for blocks and blocks hauling them on their backs. I was just about to throw out some fancy shopping bags that I got in a boutique when Mili asked me if I would give them to her instead. She uses them as handbags. "Sure," I said, and escaped to make coffee. Remedios likes a small coffee with lots of sugar. I turned on the light and there were the cockroaches, attacking the sugar. "Fuck!" I said, but quietly. Mili silently watched me. I emptied out the sugar, washed the jar, and filled it again, but this time I put it inside the fridge. "It's inevitable, you have to live with the ugly side of life," she said to me. Her pronouncement seemed to me like a defeat.

Tomorrow I'm leaving and I'm scared. Elene hasn't called… I bought some empanadas for dinner. Mili was on the computer. Reme served two bottles of wine. She stands out against the rust. She clings to the chains of memory and she survives. She could have been a model for Klimt with her dark hair. She has the power of a river that runs until it becomes a waterfall, predominant. I can imagine her at twenty, thirty, or forty, conquering the streets of Geneva, Vienna, Prague, determined to leave the mass graves behind and venture out from the stones. She has traveled so far that everything she has is piled up in her past. Milagros, on the other hand, has remained at rest, constrained by her shadow. Her face retains, like the mark of baptism, a hint of the obedient, orphaned child she no doubt was. Reme pays the bills and Mili cleans. Reme talks and Mili keeps quiet. Remedios inhales and Milagros exhales. I brush my teeth. I've been an intruder here, and yet I feel strangely at home. Another cockroach emerges from the drain, but this one is gigantic. "It's inevitable," I tell myself, and I kill it. Then, then, I turn out the light.

LOVE AT FIRST SIGHT

CELIA HAD TO LOOK for an apartment, in part because her current place was small, but mainly because she had to move out within two weeks. She was a procrastinator. Unlike you, who organized everything in advance, she enjoyed the pressure and its subsequent release. But others got trampled in the rush: they found themselves avoiding their own responsibilities to help her, always sharing in her failures, but never her success. Her ability to overcome the setbacks occasioned by her own lack of organization gave Celia a thrilling sensation of immortality that, far from driving her to repentance, made her pretentious, too stubborn to be persuaded to act any other way. And *that* was fascinating to you—so much so that you found yourself tasked with finding her an apartment in Paris, making the appointments and tours on your own. You were to call her at work only when you'd found something decent, and now it seemed that you had: a furnished apartment in Saint Germain des Prés, near *Les Deux Magots*, Sartre and Simone de Beauvoir's legendary café. You repeated these details out loud and smiled, knowing that Celia would not care less about this piece of history. In fact, she would take pride in not knowing. She understood as much about books as you did about architecture.

The two of you arrived at the dilapidated yet elegant building and, hand in hand, took a slow elevator through dark floors untouched by the sun; the musty air was so stale that Celia began to sneeze. When you staggered onto the sixth floor, almost ready to turn away, the glittering light of the apartment flooded the hallway, illuminating the silhouette of an old, hunched woman with an ashen mop of hair. She wore large glasses and was engulfed by a strong smell of marijuana. Moved more by curiosity than by interest, you entered a well-lit room with yellow walls. The 1920s furniture seemed to have been arranged for a photo shoot: the sinuous, twisting chairs, the tables with aluminum legs, and the leather sofas with zebra cushions, all gave the room the air of a museum of modern art; too posed, you thought, to make the place habitable. The woman, whose hair (as you now could see in the light) was actually a huge, flabby wig, dragged on a joint as she stated the monthly rent. You did not need to look at Celia to know that she was delighted, that she wanted that apartment with its Art Deco furnishings, but you also knew that she couldn't afford it. You sighed, tired of searching. That's when Celia took you by the hand and made the only declaration that had ever been made to you in this life: "How about you move in with me?" It was not a declaration of love precisely; you were not the marrying kind, or even one to make plans; she was far from the ideal woman. But you could not say no.

As the months went by, you wondered what in the world you were doing on this thrill ride, you who'd never liked screams or heights. You were not the impulsive type, and you didn't have big urges, not even when it came to sex. The only thing you actually liked about the apartment was Celia—not the moulded ceilings, the high windows, the wooden floors: the architectural details were not what tied you to that place, even though you tried your best to appreciate the famous chiffonier and the cut-glass tulips in the bathroom. You liked Celia's deep voice as she sang the blues on some nights, ever fewer, when she improvised on the guitar and forgot about you. You enjoyed her company even as she turned her perfect body away, the two of you lying quiet on the bed. And, above all, you liked the way she could turn your gloom into optimism, dragging you towards life, just for the fun of it, without a single thought about the future, the next day, or even the next second. You liked Celia—and only Celia—or, rather, your idea of her.

Celia, on the other hand, was irritated by your lack of style, which she mockingly called "boring," as she couldn't define it in any other way. She came into the room and took away your books, climbed on top of you and unzipped your pants, only to leap down from you after a moment, furious: "Geez! You are boring." Then she imposed an embargo on sex, which ended up being more bearable for you than for her, because you did not miss her. This was perhaps the most provocative thing about you: that you did not miss her. During those days or hours, space and time were finally yours. Nobody touched your books; no one imposed libertarian schemes on your routine. You enjoyed a break from the siege, and fantasized about walking back home from the office and finding no one waiting for you. It was like being, once again, in absolute control of all that was yours, including your clutter and your silence. Above all: your silence. Celia was a constant screamer; whether cheerful or exasperated, she shouted. But when she was furious, when she was *really* furious, she did not speak to you. And then—she hated when you used literary terms—Paris was *A Moveable Feast*.

A notice arrived from the landlady's attorney, informing you that she had died. Celia was sad as she remembered the wig. "If I were her daughter, I would have liked to keep it," she said. You looked up from your book, so that she knew you were listening, but you didn't answer. "Yes," she continued, "I'd put the wig on one of those mannequin heads, and I'd comb it lovingly every night." You felt the urge to tell her to shut up, to leave you alone, but it wasn't worth the effort. You kept reading, lying on the couch, your head resting on one of the zebra cushions. The letter mentioned children who wanted to sell the apartment they'd inherited; it explained that, as a matter of French law, tenants were to be given right of first refusal. This time Celia said nothing, but you didn't need to look at her to know what she was thinking. You knew how much she loved the apartment: the bright and airy rooms; the alabaster lamps; the view of Parisian rooftops, lofts, and attics. "We should buy it," Celia said with a sigh: "Can you imagine?" And you'd been afraid that she was going to propose.

THE COMPOSITION OF SALT

For my parents

SWEATING HAD NEVER made him as uncomfortable as crying did now. He couldn't remember ever having felt gratitude for his beard before, the thick beard that caused him to chronically perspire and that now helped him to hide his quivering lip. All his life he had sweated profusely, his shirts soaked through, his hair indiscreetly damp, and in spite of this, he had never gone through so many tissues before. "Doctor, I cry all the time," he explained, thinking to himself that if he could, he would go to that proverbial hospital in the sky and exchange his lack of self-restraint for any other malady. Something strange was happening to him. Why did growing old take him this way? There can't be many men who dream of growing old; and fewer still who have longed for it ever since childhood, like he had. At six years of age, he knew that he wanted to be a grandfather, and now, when he finally was one, he was simply spoiling it all with his crying.

He held the memory clear in his mind. They had just gotten off the truck after reaching La Paz from the mine. The city held the power that comes after a snowstorm; the hills were a brighter red and the air was colder, more translucent. Even so, with the sun at its zenith, they got thirsty. His grandfather led him by the hand to the corner to buy a thayacha: his first taste of the traditional dessert made of frozen mashua tubers and sugar. He asked, what was that funny-looking thing. And the old man said briefly, "It's mashua." The big hand held his firmly, but without crushing. It was a warm, comforting hand, a man's hand. The mashua was shaped like a root and was like ice cream. His grandfather let go of his hand to show him how to eat it and gave him a wink of encouragement. The thayacha made his hands cold.

"A little more sugar," he said.

"That enough?" The white granules dissolved into the refreshing taste that filled his mouth. The sun burned down on his face.

"Delicious, isn't it?" the old man said to him and he nodded, holding onto his hand as tight as he could. The memory of his grandfather overwhelmed him. "I'm acting like a girl," he told himself every time it happened, gazing in the mirror and looking for some kind of bodily change. Women cry more on a monthly, a yearly basis, indeed all their lives.

"I'll ask the doctor for hormones, let him give a shot of testosterone!" he said to his wife, who laughed.

He looked at his wife and was forced to abandon his physiological theories; she was a woman as strong as a noble beast and she didn't cry—she had never cried—not even when their youngest son died. They were still young themselves when their little boy fell out the window. Jumping from bed to bed, he lost his balance, collided with the window and, helped along by gravity, by the laws of motion, by physics, he fell down several stories and smashed into the concrete. Even so, his beautiful body had not been damaged, and his sweet, untroubled face still held a hint of his final game, of his recent awakening as an angel. Crying wasn't possible then, crying was like casting seaweed onto the surface of a frozen, salty ocean that would end up drowning all of them, one by one, and he wasn't going to let that happen. Crying, he felt sure, was like letting his son sink into dark waters and anchoring him to a rock just so they could see him there, eyes open, down in the depths. Why should he be crying now?

"I like your eyes better like this, you have sailor's eyes," she said to cheer him up, "ocean eyes."

"Fuck the ocean. We lost the ocean in the War of the Pacific!" he grumbled.

When he was a child, his mother had sometimes passed the night telling him stories about the Pacific Ocean, with its salt, with its chill, and with its secrets. Sometimes, she rocked him to sleep to the dark sound of that ocean, held in the spiral of a shell.

"I don't care, you have ocean eyes."

His wife wasn't bothered by his crying or by his perennially red eyes. She even envied him; she too would have liked to learn to cry, but she couldn't. She wasn't made to let it all spill out. Together they had constructed in their hearts a medieval fortress of austerity and courage, not lacking in will, nor in love, nor in guilt, and least of all in sorrow. In this way they managed to make their way through life with intention, but never completely surrendering to joy. That's how they were, a little sad, a little enigmatic, a little closed off from their ability to receive. And what he was least willing to receive was the fussing and hugging that people held out to him—without asking first, and with an exceedingly annoying familiarity—just because he was crying.

The doctor advised him not to worry.

"Crying is healthy."

"Screw healthy, doctor," he answered. "I'm too old to be healthy!"

This was a miscalculation. He had expected that old age would usher him into a state of serene invulnerability, not the opposite. Where did it come from, this newfound capacity to be overcome by anything, these bursts of rapture that made him sniffle, then sob? The worst part was the scientific optimism that knocked him against the ropes with the diagnosis that he didn't have an illness, that the reason lay deep within him. It wasn't anything like a brain injury or a birth defect, the doctor had explained; his tears weren't flowing independent of his emotions. These tears weren't meaningless, they didn't come without cause.

"The problem," he said, "is that I'm turning into a sissy."

"A real problem," his wife corrected him, "would be if you had that cat's cry syndrome the doctor was talking about. Imagine if you couldn't stop meowing instead of crying! I wouldn't sleep a wink." They both laughed.

But the problem persisted; everything moved him to tears. One afternoon he went to an event at his grandson's school and as soon as he set foot in the classroom, he clearly identified the scent of his own childhood: the smell of those little desks! He had to squeeze his eyes shut to keep the tears from bursting out. He left the school, disgusted and furious with himself. Outside it was raining. The Latin verb *plorare* means "to cry"; crying shares the same etymology as rain—in Latin, *pluvia*—rain like a squall, like a downpour, like a storm that gusted him down the road, into shortcuts and alleys, keeping clear of the line of cars that, like paper streamers, unfurled downtown as twilight gathered in the city.

Walking helped him. He passed unaware from the asphalt to the old cobblestone streets, feeling his troubles drain from him incrementally with each stride, while he began to see before him the stalls of the old Indian women who called to him now, offering to read his fortune in coca leaves. The incense and myrrh made him drowsy, dizzy with the colors of purplish wool, shiny wrappers, and sweets: he was in the witches' market. He could make out various herbs, along with dried llama fetuses and stone mortars and pestles. Charms, amulets, and medals danced in the wind. He remembered that Leucothoe had been buried alive by her father, who was enraged by her affair with Apollo. And that Apollo, to honor the dead princess, had transformed her into a luxuriant frankincense tree. "The Greeks were wise and horrible," he murmured. Or, to be more accurate, they were horribly wise. He smiled.

A few steps ahead, a slate board, serving as a sign, held an answer to his uneasiness. The words were written in colored chalk, in a hand that seemed imprecise rather than childish: "Cures for spiritual fright, cleansing baths for joy," he read, and he entered into a dark room of tall adobe walls, where an ancient woman with a curved spine gave him his prescription: a bath in the ocean, with his eyes open. He asked her sarcastically if perhaps she wasn't aware that they lived in a landlocked country. To which she, with utmost composure, did not respond. He left, thinking about his grandson, his wife, the ocean. He was drenched and starting to feel cold. The night had draped, like an enormous sheet, over the city. Once again he was miserable. What could he do? Why was it suddenly so hard to breathe? What would he need to change to escape a breakdown? He grew ashamed of his thoughts and felt the urge to apologize, but his wife wasn't with him and wouldn't be home until late. In the end, she was the only thing that mattered . . .

That night, in the darkened apartment, as he started a hot bath to avoid catching cold, he began to think he understood what the old woman had been trying to tell him. The size of the ocean didn't matter, it just had to be salt water. So he ran to the kitchen with gusto, then returned and dumped a whole jar of coarse salt into the bathtub. His wife would scold him, he knew it, but that wasn't important. Then he paused a few moments before turning on the water. He wasn't entirely sure if it should be cold or hot, but decided on the latter. "Let's say it's the Caribbean," he told himself, and the sight of the filling tub reassured him. It was as if reality had resolved into coherence. Standing naked by the tub, he stepped in quickly, yearning to weep underwater. He felt that he knew where it was all coming from, and he was ready to confront it. Then he immersed himself in the salty liquid of his ocean, with his eyes closed. He waited until he was ready to open his eyes, and then he did, but he didn't see his son anywhere. Dismayed, he returned to the surface. He took a deep breath and, without conscious thought, immersed himself again, searching for an image, for some kind of meaning. But this time he curled up on his left side and stayed that way for a long time, holding his breath. The water was still warm when he began to be rocked by the faraway sound of the ocean, held in the spiral of a shell.

THE RED RIBBON

NATALIA ARRIVED AT the bar late, but we cut her some slack, because she brought a story with her. This time my sister didn't even apologize for being late; she knew an hour or two wasn't all that much to us. After all, we're the press and, at the local bar, waiting is never a problem. She sat down and started talking (a very rare occurrence, since she usually sits quietly and listens to Gabriel, whose intelligence overshadows everything and everyone else). I like the timbre of her voice. I don't know what it is about her soft and indifferent tone that soothes me. But this time her voice was not serene; she had just left the paper and still throbbed with the urgency of midnight ink. "A man's been arrested," she blurted out. Natalia appeared anxious, so we asked her if the man was innocent. She responded with something of an apology: "I don't know," she said, and she took Gabriel's hand in hers.

She shared what she knew for a fact: Rebecca had been crowned Carnival Queen, and now Rebecca was dead. Natalia had been given photographs of both the murder scene and the parade. We were thus able to mentally reconstruct that cheap carnival, haphazardly erected in the sand and trash on the outskirts of the city. Rebecca had not enjoyed her fifteen minutes of fame, having been killed before the festivities. As Natalia told us the story of her fleeting reign, we imagined an indigenous community living in unspeakable poverty, a community that, just like the girl, was inexorably headed toward extinction. Gabriel kissed Natalia on the forehead, a second before my sister let go of his hand and said, not without a touch of drama: "No one could have imagined what destiny had in store for the Queen, least of all the people who crowned her."

That day had been so bright: a hair-loose-and-smooth and easy-laughter kind of day. The red carnation tied to the waistband of her short shorts accentuated Rebecca's wide hips. She was fourteen, but she had stopped being a child long ago. It was possible she hadn't experienced childhood at all, born straight into adulthood, I thought, while Natalia reported what the experts had told her, that the girl had come from a concupiscent culture. We tried to figure out what the experts meant by "concupiscent" and we translated it like this: an Amazonian people—hunters, nomads, weavers—for whom carnal virtues are cardinal virtues. This was still very abstract. We imagined maternal breasts, female songs, young girls initiated into the pleasures of the flesh. In their world, Natalia said, time and space are part of the oral tradition; lust and pleasure are not seen as sinful but as natural, vital. For a few seconds, her explanation took us to Paradise, and then to Hell, because when that indigenous reality collides with city life, freedom becomes a yoke dragging women into the world's oldest meat grinder. Poverty grinds it all up: at an unimaginably young age, Indian girls surrender their bodies to urban fantasies for next to nothing. "How much exactly?" I asked. Natalia answered without poetry: "Two pesos."

Her weary voice made me think of snow, of my skin aching in the cold, of ice melting into water. Of La Paz. Unlike Rebecca, I'd outgrown my childhood only late in life, when I followed my sister to La Paz to go to college. It is true that I wasn't precisely a child then, but I was from a small town. My adolescence was a sheltered one, and I endured it like a disease. Seventeen is a bit late for a city girl, but not for a country girl who's both too insulated and too eager to jump.

I can't say that I spread my wings like a dove ready for flight. I knew even then that the wind wouldn't carry me; the effort would have to be all mine. Prudence was not one of my virtues, particularly in those days, when I refused to compromise my glorious freedom by planning ahead. My flight was to be a fierce, aerodynamic, choppy one: a violent leap into the unknown, storming the city, grasping at all those things I was dying to see and experience. Yes, I've got my demons, but there is no one to blame for what happened except me. And even though Natalia often reproaches herself for taking me to the city, the truth is that the decision was mine, and mine alone. The only thing I still resent her for is saving me when I wanted to die. She scraped some snow from the roof of a car and put it on my cheeks to try to keep me conscious, both the snow and her voice becoming more and more disembodied: "What's wrong, baby? What have they done to you? What am I going to tell Mom and Dad?" And my own voice: "Nothing. Promise me."

Natalia went on with her story. Rebecca had gotten picked up by a taxi driver who asked her if she wanted to go for a ride. Another girl, Angelica, the last person to see Rebecca alive, reported all this. The two of them wanted to go together, but

Angelica was very pregnant, and the taxi driver refused to let her in. "Pregnant?" someone (I don't remember who) asked, as if they couldn't believe it. Instinctively, I looked away. Natalia confirmed: Yes, the taxi driver didn't want her in his car, even though he'd been with her days before. He was a regular at the Pampas. "And what was he like?" someone asked. "Fat," Natalia said. Well, more potbellied than fat. Old. Tall. Angelica had been precise: Like a grandfather. White, just like the taxi. Almost sweet. He probably paid more than two pesos because the girls fought each other a little to climb into his cab, and besides that he always bought them an ice cream. But that afternoon—or should we call it evening?—it was about seven o'clock and the sky was still light when he chose the Queen because she was the prettiest. Rebecca was more than pretty. You could see it in the picture that Natalia showed us. The girl was hot and pink and juicy like the heart of a watermelon. "A hundred-degree fever," Gabriel said.

Gabriel avoided me, the way you cross the street when you don't want to say hello to someone you know has already seen you. He watched my hands out of the corner of his eye, responded to whatever I said with complete silence, and no one noticed, except for Natalia and me. When I was a child, he saw me as a spoiled brat who provoked both irritation and tenderness. I was about four, maybe five, when Gabriel started taking Natalia out. They weren't exactly a couple yet, but it was so natural to see them together, just like now. Gabriel would come by in the evenings, firing off his sarcastic jokes with the precision of a slingshot. Natalia would grab my hands away from my face: "Stop picking your nose, you pig!" But I couldn't resist, and I pushed my finger all the way up my nostril. I was on a mission to taste that forbidden fruit, and my sister was on a mission to catch me doing it. Gabriel had no idea, for Natalia would never have told on me; but how could I know that back then? He was unaware of many things, including the power of language. He came to our house during the siesta, while I played on the veranda floor, wrapped up in myself. "Hey there, snot-nose," he said. Seeing his eyes on the tip of my finger, I burst into tears. Natalia couldn't contain herself. "You're so, so mean," I shouted. Gabriel didn't understand and my sister doubled over with laughter: "He's just teasing you, silly; don't take it literally."

Someone asked again about Rebecca, wanting to take a psychological approach. Natalia held back and allowed us to theorize. How to describe her without flattening her out? Joyful and extroverted, we supposed, because she wouldn't have been crowned Queen otherwise. But we also agreed that there are different ways of being joyful. One person might possess a bodily joy, an electric, aggressive temperament destined to be worn down by life and the passage of time. Others possess a more rational, almost routine joy: that quality, more decisive than destiny, that we vaguely call optimism. We agreed that Rebecca's joy must have been a little intransigent; that is to say, it persisted in spite of everything, in spite of the horrors in her life. In which case it must also have been illogical; and then, who knows, Rebecca's extroversion may have been a mask, a defense mechanism. It seemed more appropriate for a girl of her age to be timid, quietly cheerful, sensitive to the unexpected. For her, just about anything would have been unexpected: a new dress, a table with a tablecloth, hot water, going to school, receiving a gift without having to give herself in return. We ran out of words.

Natalia said that nobody noticed Rebecca was missing until the police found her by the side of the road, in the underbrush. No one was looking for her because Rebecca, her grandmother said, was like a cat: she disappeared for a while, but she always returned. Rebecca liked going places, Angelica said; she liked to get lost. "Who doesn't like to get lost?" I thought, hugging myself in the freezing air conditioning. That's why she carried a little tin of Hercules superglue in her handbag, ready for long distances. When they identified her body in the morgue, Rebecca no longer looked like a queen: she'd lost her short shorts and her red carnation, and her long straight hair was a tangled mat. Her body had been covered with a jute bag, probably a potato sack. Her grandmother passed her hands all over Rebecca's body, without tears, as if performing a ritual. She understood that death requires no explanations, even as the sergeant did his duty, arriving at a hypothesis of strangulation (he could not say for certain whether the girl had been raped). Angelica told Natalia that her friend's body was smeared with superglue, the same kind she carried in her purse, so much of it that you could hardly make out her tattoos, the heart, the lizard, the star. "The flesh is sorrowful," I whispered. Mallarme's poem was so true.

Gabriel nudged Natalia to change the subject when the story became explicit, but our absolute silence encouraged her to continue. "Journalism is like an immunological disease," he offered as an apology. "Sometimes you can inoculate yourself," Natalia rejoined, "but sometimes you just have to let yourself get sick." Natalia couldn't stop fighting with Gabriel, even though her victories were insignificant, like having the last word, cleverly finishing a sentence, or generally being much more attractive and charming than he was. Suddenly I noticed how very tired she looked. She hadn't slept well for the last few days and, consequently, Gabriel hadn't either. During her pro-longed insomnia, she tried to mentally reconstruct Rebecca's murder, but it was impossible. Gabriel had been supportive at the beginning, but he'd given up: "Go to sleep, go to sleep, woman." Gabriel laughed. We all laughed, even Natalia, who by then was as freezing as I was.

When they opened up another couple bottles of beer and

started filling the glasses, I escaped to the bathroom. I sat down on the toilet, comforted by the warm, suffocating microclimate inside the stall, untouched by the bar's artificial winter. Only for a race like ours was this kind of curiosity possible—scientific, but also a little morbid—allowing us to speak of rape and death without losing our appetite. I pinched my cheeks in front of the mirror after rinsing my face. Natalia was strong enough for this kind of story. I knew it all too well. She had been there for me, carrying me on her back, dragging me to the bus stop, because we had no money, then soothing my fever with wet rags and mumbling between her prayers: "Crazy. Fucking crazy. Hail Mary, full of grace ... "

I went back to the table, where the story continued.

Not much time had passed—at least not from the official, investigative point of view—between the discovery of Rebecca's body and the police being forced to arrive at the gates of the community to apprehend the culprit. "Fifteen hours at most," Natalia said. Her choice of verb was deliberate: the police really were "forced" to come because the community was not willing to wait for the leisurely unfolding of "official" and "investigative" procedures. Fifteen hours—in a country where justice can take centuries. "But of course," Natalia said, "time never works in favor of the condemned ... " It hadn't in my case: as the doctors put it, everything might have been different if I had been seen just a few hours earlier. Those few hours haunted Natalia, even now. She had lost all sense of time, and in the end it was Gabriel who had forced her to leave the room, called a taxi and dragged us to the hospital. I was ashen, as cold as a corpse; my sister was frail and trembling, her eyes emptied by weariness and the horror of all that blood.

By three o'clock in the morning, we were the only ones left in the bar. The photographer spoke, giving the tale its epilogue: "We're so used to this shit," he said, "no one should be surprised by how fast it all went down. But are you telling me you're going to accept the way they identified the killer?" According to what certain anonymous witnesses had told Natalia, the women were sitting together on the broken curb when a boy came up to them. He was freshly bathed, his shirt tucked into his pants, with some kind of wooden board in his hands. Without saying a word, guided by their knowing, they gave each other a sidelong glance, like birds. The boy even smiled at them before he asked for Rebecca. And they responded to him in chorus, with violent shouts, attracting a mob: drunken men blinded by alcohol, hungry for blood. At this point Natalia condensed the tale: they hung the boy from a lamppost, whose yellow rays outlined his body like a spotlight. And what happened next was indeed a form of theater. Men, women and children surrounded the crucified body, exorcising their fury as if this were their Carnival. But instead of dancing, they were striking him with stones, sticks and belts, in the name of the dead Queen.

Gabriel said that when the police lowered him from the lamppost, the boy was half dead, his head and body smashed and his clothes reduced to rags. Natalia added a sentimental note: Angelica still had the wooden board. He had brought as a present for Rebecca, a cutting board for her grandmother's kitchen. He was a carpenter, she said, eighteen years old and five and a half feet tall. In his statement, he confessed to having paid for Rebecca twice. As they spoke, Gabriel and Natalia looked like a couple of television newscasters. They complemented each other perfectly. No wonder they'd had three children together. Not one but three. And every time she got pregnant, my sister looked at me with guilty eyes, as if she wanted to avoid hurting me, even though I'd told her not to worry, that I was happy for her.

"A clock strikes at the heart of every newspaper," Natalia said. She said it a little before closing time, that night when she had to file her profile of a murderer without believing a word. "He could have easily been an innocent bystander," she had told her editor; but she confessed to us that she just didn't know. Her face held a cloud of remorse, even though her words were resigned. She had done her job. Isaac Chingano, Saul Rosales, Roque Pando, Juan Bustos, Juana Nomine, the prosecutor, the investigator, the village cacique, the grandmother, everyone she talked to told her that the case was closed, that the community had spoken, that justice had been done because the culprit had been caught. "Of course they needed to catch someone," Gabriel said. Someone whose sacrifice would smooth the waters and allow them to keep on living. "Someone to save them," I thought, just like Natalia had always saved me. Just like she wanted to do now, trying to convince Gabriel to let her carry my baby for me.

They finally turned off the air conditioning, and as they did, there was a clear, almost echoing silence. I felt as if the lights had been switched on in a darkened room. Then Gabriel asked, "But how did they know it was him? What reason did they give?" And Natalia answered with a bitter smile. They knew it was him because they had bound a red ribbon on Rebecca's left foot, to bring the murderer forward, and he was the first one to come asking for her. "And then what did you do?" I asked, unfairly, as if my sister was supposed to have the answer for everything. "I just wrote the story," Natalia responded, "as best I could."

THE GIRL

I

THE GIRL HAD LEFT THE table in a hurry, and although the others feigned indifference, they couldn't conceal their curiosity for long. With dinner at an end and the coffee cups half empty, they came around to the only subject that remained both untouched and unavoidable. Eda, for one, couldn't wait to bring it up.

"Well," she said. "Looks like you've broken the mold this time, haven't you?"

The corners of their mouths twitched.

"It's no big deal, Eda," Blas said with a forced smile.

"You're such a puritan," Duke told her.

"Here you go again! We can't say shit ever since you've become an ecologist."

"Ecologist" was what Eda called anyone who was being politically correct. Of late, this seemed to particularly annoy her, as did Duke himself.

"Tell the truth, Eda. What are you most upset about?"

Duke asked, and with his usual power of synthesis, he added: "the tattoos, or the fact that she's a spic?"

Blas, who'd been playing with his napkin, looked up to weigh the impact of these words on Eda.

"Don't exaggerate." Eda turned to her right and lightly touched Blas's hand clutching his napkin. "Blas, forgive me for saying this, but that girl is trash. End of story."

"End of story?" Duke laughed and patted Blas on the shoulder. "Don't mind her! That girl is smoking hot, man. And one more thing—" This time he raised his right eyebrow, looking straight at Eda: "She's more worldly than anyone at this table."

The girl, whom they would never call by name, had many more tattoos than were visible to the naked eye. It's true she was gorgeous, so Eda had tried her best not to undress her with her eyes. But she'd caught a glimpse of the bird spread out across the nape of her neck. "It's Maori," the girl had explained with a wink, well aware of Eda's curiosity. Duke, the forever brazen one, took to staring openly whenever Blas ran his fingers over the snake curled like a ring around the girl's finger. As for Blas, he got an erection every time he considered the crown of flowers that hugged the girl's knee and traveled down her calf to reach her ankle.

Blas was not a guy with a lot of experience. And, for Eda, that was precisely the problem: he lacked street smarts; anyone could deceive him. Sweet as he was, trusting and open as he was, what a pity that he gave in to the very first girl to show him serious interest! Eda didn't care that the girl might be a gold digger—although in truth she didn't appear to be—because Blas was well off and many others had gone after his money before, without leaving him hanging out to dry. With the others, though, Blas had been tender and flirty, and even a little vulnerable, but in the end he never lost his lucidity. He enjoyed showing them off, although he didn't seem to take them to bed very often; the girls drank summer drinks, occupied the dressing rooms at the mall, and then disappeared when either they or Blas got bored. They'd all been out of the same mold: bottle blondes with careful haircuts and shapely figures, cardigans casually knotted around their necks. Slightly prudish, they spoke little, and when they did open their mouths, it left much to be desired. Eda ambushed them, and later laughed at their expense. With the last one, it went something like this:

"But what the fuck got into you, asking her about the economy?" Duke scolded her.

"I never thought she'd take it so seriously," Eda said, faking embarrassment. "Blas, you'll forgive me, right?"

And Blas had joined in their laughter, acknowledging that he could never have seen himself growing old with someone who expressed herself thusly: "Well, even if the economic crisis doesn't directly affect you, it still does affect you. I mean, I can see how bad some people have it. I'm not talking about myself or anything, but I do have friends, people from good families, who are totally broke now, you know?" (Blas could not believe that she was still talking.) "And that's even worse than it is for bums who have always been out on the street—poor souls, but at least they're used to it... " (Did she seriously just refer to them as "poor souls"?) "Poverty is only a real problem for people who know what it's like to live comfortably, and all of a sudden they're losing their home and their job. That is the real tragedy!"

The girl, the new girl that is, couldn't be written off so easily. You noticed her miles away, even in the heart of a city like Barcelona. She was so different that Blas began to imagine their life together, using the plural to speak of his plans—"we" or "we're going to" or "we are"—which infuriated Eda and touched Duke, who was secretly relieved that Blas could finally stop being the third wheel. The girl, for one, had no patience for etiquette or the rules set by society; she was anything but intimidated by the ethical, aesthetic, or intellectual formalities of a world in which she knew she was an outsider. She was intelligent but distracted. She wasn't afraid to laugh at herself or at others, especially at Eda. It was quite clear that she wasn't made to sit quietly and look pretty; for starters, she didn't keep a lid on anything. And that was what Blas liked best, her noisy presence, her lack of respect for personal space, and most of all the way she sucked out the oxygen around Eda, extinguishing her light.

"You shouldn't trust her," Eda said. "Just look into her eyes and you'll know that she's crazy. She told us herself that she drove her first husband insane. She almost killed him, and here you are now: offering yourself up like a sacrificial lamb."

"The guy was loco, Eda, and a real scumbag," Duke interjected. "If she hadn't shot him, he'd have killed her. What else could she do?" Blas was silent.

"Only a madwoman marries a loon!" Eda wailed.

Over time, Blas felt a quiet relief as Eda's jabs at the girl lost their power. What seemed to Eda to be a sign of insanity, Blas and Duke accepted as part of the girl's exuberant personality. But this didn't stop Eda from mumbling. A tattooed scalp hiding under a shock of hair—was that not pathological? The girl had given her two-year old son a tattoo as a symbol of their "spiritual connection"—didn't she belong in a psych ward? How is it that a mother, who speaks three languages and has a college degree, leaves her child behind with his grandparents, on another continent, to try her luck bartending on the beach? "Fuck it, she's crazy!" Eda repeated. But her words had become unobtrusive, like rain.

"She doesn't like me, does she? If I were going to be childish about it, I'd even say that she hates me," the girl, faced with Eda's disapproval, mused from time to time.

"Nonsense. She doesn't hate you. Eda is difficult, but she's not that kind of person. Don't take it the wrong way."

"No, I'm not taking it the wrong way." The girl added with a touch of malice, "The poor thing is so—" Blas held his breath, waiting for the blow.

"Stuck up? Is that the word?" He smiled, nodding, and she let out a deep laugh. "She's got a stick up her ass." As she spoke, Blas watched her lips move, so appetizingly vulgar. The girl galvanized him, and he was eager to possess her.

"Come on, forget Eda. You'll get used to each other."

And Eda had no other choice than to get used to the situation. It was either that or get used to not seeing Blas, who no longer took her phone calls. However, her forced acquiescence didn't make it easier for her to embrace the girl, nor did it stop her from cooking up all kinds of mischief aimed at ridiculing her or getting rid of her entirely. Eda couldn't stop herself, even though her powers of ingenuity seemed to wane as she saw her influence on Blas shrink to nothing.

In any case, Duke was the first to see the writing on the wall. Not that it wasn't obvious after a while: Blas was getting married, and a certain someone would have to accept it. It was as if Blas needed to prove to Eda and to the world that he was a real man, that he could handle a girl of her caliber. That's why, in Eda's opinion and to the girl's delight, he planned a hopelessly tacky wedding. Everything was kitschy and drenched in symbolism, from the gold and fuchsia chair covers to the white doves released at the end of the ceremony. Christmas lights dangled from every tree, and an overpowering scent of incense filled the air. Blas, in his tuxedo, glowed with self-satisfaction. He couldn't stop talking about their honeymoon plans. The girl had set her heart on a voyage to the Amazon. And that was something none of his friends could fathom: Blas in a canoe, surrounded by alligators, mosquitoes, and bioluminescent plants. But postcards from Blas soon arrived as proof: he'd overcome his childhood fears and submerged himself in that muddy river called Madre de Dios, surrounded by pink dolphins with foreheads like melons. "Unbelievable" was how Eda put it.

"Extraordinary" was how Blas himself put it. The girl, who believed that the river could cure everything, threw her naked body into the water, swam with the dolphins, and then splashed on the banks until her hair, shoulders, and entire body were covered with mud and clouds of insects. The insects were dangerous, Blas reminded her, as he watched the sunlight gleaming on her curves. Blas believed he could see the movements of a divine hand: one from which he ate turtle eggs, wild boar, piranha, ants, mashed cassava and sweet potato; one from which he drank brandy, sugarcane juice and, with the guidance of a shaman, a hallucinogenic brew of sacred flowering vines, which caused him to shit and puke all night long, as a form of purification.

II

When they returned from their honeymoon, Blas took the girl straight to an apartment he'd rented in Horta Guinardó, near Gaudí's Park Güell, because he wanted to surprise her and he thought that, very soon, her son could come live with them and they'd take him to the park to play. Blas had even spoken with the child's grandparents. But the girl became infuriated, considering it an ambush. She made quite the scene.

"I will not allow you to control my life!" she screamed. "And don't you mess with my son."

Blas—who wasn't the type to beg—begged this time, promising her that they would do everything her way: from grocery lists to vacation plans. The girl did not respond. From music selections to holiday menus. Still, an icy silence. From contraception to home decor. Nothing. Then Blas got down on his knees. Movies and walks, towels and pets: everything would be the way she liked it. At last, the girl laughed. She'd taken her sweet time, but in the end she granted him the forgiveness he yearned for, absolving herself from guilt and earning the right, in Eda's words, "to fill the apartment with crap." She hung brightly patterned sarongs over the tasteful paintings that Blas favored, and covered the white armchairs with colorful Andean textiles. An elaborate wire ornament dangled from every lamp, and to these she attached images of the Buddha, self-help mottos, and suicidal poems that Eda couldn't even bring herself to laugh at: now she was worried for real.

"Who puts shit like that in their house?"

"Let it go, Eda," Duke said. "She puts them up when she's not feeling well. The girl gets migraines."

"When this thing goes south—and it will—I'll be the one with the migraines," Eda told him. "You guys can see it coming, but you've chosen to turn a blind eye. Blas is nothing but a puppet," she mumbled, while she rinsed out the lettuce for Sunday brunch.

After a few months, however, Duke and Eda no longer thought it necessary to speak their minds, because Blas seemed to be recovering his sanity. He had returned from his last business trip powered up like a freight train, determined to settle into what he called a "masterful" life, to be lived according to his own tastes and desires. This was the Blas they knew. He even got the girl to leave her job at the beach bar and convinced her to take on some translation jobs offered by Duke.

"Do it for me, babe," he said.

"Who else would I be doing it for?" she answered, lying on the couch, looking ill.

In the same way, he put an end to the small things. He started with the kitchen and then swept through the entire apartment. One day he packed all the tassels, mirrors, and ornaments into a box, saying he was going to repaint the walls. The box later disappeared.

"Jesus, it's all so... clinical," Duke joked one night. Eda kicked him under the table. Pretending not to hear, Blas passed around the glasses of wine, but the girl jumped on Duke's remark.

"I've never believed in minimalism," she said, her face deathly pale. "Sadly, this goes beyond the decor. Blas has lost his spine, and I'm deeply confused." This time nobody laughed.

But it shouldn't have been a surprise. Blas had never liked ethnic flourishes, and the girl was apparently the only one unaware of it. Now her fire was dying, a little more every day, as she began to see Blas in a different light. To his credit, when Blas noticed certain changes in the girl, he made an effort to rein himself in. For example, the evenings still belonged to her. At the end of each day, they walked on the rivers of lava in Park Güell, between the columns shaped like trees. They always stopped by the glass and ceramic mosaics, which fascinated the girl, reminding her of the Amazon. Blas never rushed her, even though, compared to the tremolo of life and work in the city, he found himself profoundly bored by the lizard eyes, the orchids, the brightly colored birds. The girl stroked the colorful fragments, traced the mortar with her fingers, and remained bewitched and silent. Sometimes those moments precipitated a plunge into the abyss of a terrible migraine.

The girl's silences—at first sporadic, but soon prolonged—irritated Blas. The magic was fading, and so was his admittedly limited patience. He found himself wanting to shake her, to get her to snap out of it; regretfully he remembered Eda's many words of warning. But Blas only dared to vent his frustrations to Duke:

"Man, there's nothing she wants anymore... "

The girl didn't eat, sleep, or bathe anymore, and she didn't want sex. The only thing she did do was smoke, her eyes like the polka dots on the white sheets of their bed.

"Jesus, not even her headaches are like a normal person's," was Eda's remark, behind Blas's back.

She experienced skull-splitting pains that left her lying in the darkened apartment, all day, all night, and into the next day. What was odd was that the pains were noisy.

"It's like a hundred bees buzzing inside my head!" the girl sobbed to Blas. "They keep getting louder and louder, like insects swarming in the rainforest."

Blas didn't know whether he should believe her, offer her a joint, or simply ignore the outbursts. He couldn't remember what the rainforest sounded like. Far from it: he wouldn't have been able to identify a cicada if his life depended on it. How was he supposed to stay calm within her deafening storm?

"Wait and see, they won't be able to find anything wrong with her," Eda said. But Blas was too tired to respond, and Duke was silent.

At the hospital, the girl bawled ceaselessly. Blas would have preferred a tragic, fatal diagnosis, but the doctors prescribed sedatives and pronounced her strange condition to be all in her head, triggering another avalanche of doubts.

This was Blas's worst nightmare: standing in line at the pharmacy, begging for opiates.

"I should have smacked the crap out of you," Eda said. "That would have saved you from this psycho." Now that she had regained some of her influence, joyful tenderness had replaced her usual scolding. Duke, fired up with anger at Eda, sided with the girl.

But the girl did nothing to help her case, lost as she was in an inexhaustible flood of tears. One day she shaved her head in an attempt to root out the pain. Blas found himself repulsed by the sight of her tattooed skull.

"I'm not going to say I told you so." This, naturally, from Eda.

"No, you're much too classy," Duke observed.

"Back off," Blas said.

Duke felt the urge to hit him, to abort the impending birth of the past, but he didn't have the guts. After all, Eda had already offered Blas their guest room.

III

The girl would have liked to hurt Blas, even if only physically—something like a stab, a scratch in the eye, or a bite—as if leaving him with a visible, festering wound would somehow assuage her sense of shame and defeat.

"You bastard, you're leaving me now that I'm ugly!" was the only thing that occurred to her to say. Blas would later try to forget her sobs, the way one tries to forget the discomfort of a venereal disease.

"Fine, go back to Ms. Perfect," she spit out. "You'll grow old with Eda, but you'll never want to fuck her! Especially not

70

with that other moron always hanging around like her pimp!"

Blas was already leaving when the girl screamed again, hurling one glass ashtray after another against the door.

"Traitor!" she groaned with the fury of all the waters—hurricanes and storms and tropical rivers—until she was left dry and barren, with another migraine.

Duke would later maintain that he was the one who had rescued the girl from her silence. Blas knew him well enough not to question him, while Eda retorted that Duke wasn't the type to rescue his own mother. And yet, they both knew that Duke had gone to see the girl.

It was mid-afternoon, when sunlight still filtered through the blinds, and the sound of the doorbell had forced the girl to open her eyes. Struggling up from the couch, she set her bare feet on the floor and cut one of her soles on the scattered shards of glass. Hopping around on the other foot, she went to open the door and found herself face to face with Duke, who had dropped by to pay her for her translations.

"It's you. What do you want?"

Duke described to Blas and Eda how he closed the door behind him, then carefully swept the broken glass to the wall with the tip of his shoe.

"What a sight," Duke said. "Aren't those the crystal ashtrays that Eda gave you guys? Oy! They cost her a fortune."

The girl didn't answer. She sat still for a while, looking around for her sandals.

"What have you done to yourself? Let me help you." Duke went to the medicine cabinet and cleaned off her foot, but the cut was deep.

"Let's go to the hospital. I'll take you."

The girl got angry. "Over my dead body," she said.

She was no longer bald. She was beautiful, Duke told them, and Blas's face contorted into a grimace, not a smile. Her thick black hair had grown back enough to cover her tattoos and hide the deep scratch marks on her scalp.

"Are you still in pain?" Duke asked, touching her temple.

The girl, staring at the closed blinds, said that it didn't matter anyway. But then she admitted that the noise was still there, that she could feel her veins bulging and bursting inside her skull, and that she imagined all kinds of horrors during her sleepless nights. She also said that maybe Eda was right, that maybe she was crazy. Duke felt remorseful and promised the girl he would help her. She just closed her eyes, letting her body sway back and forth. Finally, he said goodbye.

When Blas returned to the apartment in Horta Guinardó, he found it trashed. He also found a transcontinental plane ticket on his credit card statement. He knew the girl wasn't crossing the ocean in order to return to her village or to be with her son. He knew she would rather have died than risk being seen by her child in that state. And he was right; Duke's report confirmed it. Disoriented though she was, the girl knew that she didn't want her son to remember her as a madwoman, groaning in pain. The only thing she did want was to throw herself into the river.

What happened next became part of the myth that Blas and Duke would grow to revere, just as Eda would grow to despise it. The girl had climbed onto a barge and made her way down the river, drunk as a skunk, until the boatmen dumped her insensible body on a steep bank, where she was taken in by an old man.

"I guess there's a God for the nutcases," Eda said.

As the girl explained in her letter to Duke, she only opened her eyes because she was overpowered by the tobacco smoke on her face. The old man grabbed her neck with strong hands, lifting her up as if she were weightless. Blas remembered a pair of knotty hands, an incomprehensible language, the taste of a bitter and nauseating drink. The girl, suspended in the cosmos of the jungle.

"This part you won't believe," Duke said, his face twisting with disgust, or perhaps with remorse. "The old man cut into her scalp and pulled out hundreds of larvae and fat, wriggling worms. She said just like that, the buzzing disappeared."

Eda paled. Duke, who believed he knew her well, saw that she recognized her defeat. And Blas knew that when the girl's pain disappeared into the old man's yellow eyes, whatever love they had shared had vanished with it. Then he felt pathetic, drinking coffee with Duke and Eda.

MENGELE IN LOVE

And if you like I can inject
something that we both suspect
will make your body a perfect
glass ornament.
—KLAUS & KINSKI

THE MANAGER KISSED her. It was the first time in all those years, an awkward brushing of lips that unfolded calmly, slowly. Stunned, yet unresisting, María let it happen, giving in to the man's primitive, impenetrable impulse. She squeezed her eyes closed, as if trying to shut out the light; she couldn't believe that they were in his office, and not in one of the guest bathrooms. When she opened her eyes again, he was looking at her. Feeling herself shrink under his sharp, cold gaze, she hurried away to the changing rooms. A little later, adjusting her uniform, she asked herself if she should still keep calling him "sir." But she already knew the answer. It would have made her so happy to call him "my darling," to whisper a love song into his ear, to hold him in her arms, but..."What if he fires me?" she thought, as the gentle chime of the elevator broke into her daydream.

Arami, a five-star hotel has its charms, believe me. If you were here I'd show you around, without the manager finding out, I'd show you everything. I know how much you'd love it, all of it: the thick carpeting—"imperial," they say it's called; the floor-to-ceiling mirrors, not like that cracked, spotty thing we used to have in our bedroom; the vanilla merengues, in big glass bowls, that anyone can take for free; all the little twinkling lights, even though it's nowhere near Christmas; and the elevator, oh, if you could only see the elevator, Arami, you never stepped into anything like it, girl...

María, whose job it was to clean the guest rooms floor by floor, believed that the elevator was the greatest of the hotel's many charms. She had her reasons: pushing that heavy cart, piled high with towels, spray bottles, and rags, was hard work. Dear God, she could feel every one of her 66 years. It was hard work; but no, she thought, what did she have to complain about? After all, the hotel was full of beautiful things, and she had lived through so much ugliness; and her job was fine, even on the days when the manager made her cry, although sometimes, like today, the days were... Never mind. Better not to think about it.

In the beginning, back when she had just started at the hotel, María used to call the elevator to go down a floor and think about how elegant the buttons were: flat, not round, and shiny steel, not plastic. She hated round elevator buttons like the ones in her apartment building; some joker was always trying to set them on fire with a lighter, and over time the surface got dark and dirty. If she could only clean them... That's right, like she did at the hotel, with all of those sprays and chemicals parceled out by the manager, who was tall, had light brown hair, and was always in a rush, who spoke Spanish with a hard

Teutonic edge that made it difficult for her to understand him, no matter how closely she listened.

But it's not just the hotel that you'd like, Arami; and if you could only see him with your own eyes, you would know exactly what I mean. You'd be reminded of him, sister. It's impossible to see him and not remember. He talks just like Fritz, I swear it, just like when you were teaching him, back home in the village.

And this was true: in another time, another country, Arami had taught another man a few words of Guaraní, as if he were blind. With dramatic gestures, she brought his large, white, heavy hands to her lips: "*Voi potá* means *I love you*," she told him. He pushed her onto the metal table, tied down her arms, held her head hard underneath the light, and then bent his face close, so close to hers that their eyelashes brushed together.

María sighed, thinking about the buttons: if she could only clean them… Cleaning was a way to erase the filth from her existence. "Cleaning is healing!" She had been told this many times by her sister Arami, her twin. They were identical except for Arami's eyes, one green and one blue, like a *quesú* cat: "*Quesú* means *bad*," said Arami. Maybe that's why María had come to adore, of all things, the smell of bleach. As she liked to say, you can bleach away anything, even blood—anything, that is, except love. Sweat stains disappear from clothes; the fluids of another body melt away from your skin… This she had learned when she was still a girl. A woman's body can smell like new again. Memories can be bleached away in a basin of soapy water. You just immerse yourself like a dirty shirt, then scrub hard all over, and that does the trick. If you could only gargle with bleach. One time, back home in the village, María drank a glassful of bleach because a man—that man—didn't love her, had never loved her. But she survived. She woke up in the hospital with her esophagus badly burned. "Spiteful girl," was the first thing she heard when she opened her eyes. It was Arami's voice: "Spiteful!"

There was no need for that, Arami. All I wanted was to get out of your way. Don't forget, this was long before he left the village. Before all of those angry people arrived, asking questions, taking photos, and filming. Those people came from far away, Arami, but you never saw them, because you left us the very same night that he told you goodbye.

She ran her hands over the elevator buttons, thinking how much she liked them. Anything smooth is beautiful! Long straight hair, the scent of recently ironed cloth, the surface of a freshly made bed, the floor of the elevator... It was marble, shiny and perfect, much easier to roll the cart across than the hospital linoleum. María had worked in a hospital once. There, the elevators weren't modernized: no music, no emergency intercom system, no lights. Well, not like the lights in the elevator of a five-star hotel, which to María's eyes were as bright as stage lights, and held no lingering, rusty odor of blood. Besides, this elevator was so wide that she could fit the whole cart in without being squeezed off to the side; there was plenty of room for her to look at herself in the full-length mirrors. María looked up and let the stage lights bathe her face. She knew something about the stage—about singing, really. She liked to sing in the shower, and in the elevator. Well, as for actual singing, only in the shower. In the elevator, she just moved her lips to the words. Otherwise, someone might hear her. And María's job mattered to her. It mattered to her even more than the manager, who she liked so much, and yet, didn't know how to talk to.

One day, the man that Arami called "Uncle Fritz" appeared in their village. Later, after his sudden departure, people told stories: he liked to inject people in the eyes; he used to boil children alive; his backyard was a shallow graveyard. She didn't know why they talked about him that way. She only knew that he had heavy hands, was a doctor, and knew how to leave his perfect seed inside her. Arami whispered in his ear *"Rojaijo,"* which meant much more than "I love you," because he had chosen her over María. It must have been because of her eyes; like a bad cat's, they had a touch of the devil about them. "Arami, my little blue sky," he sang to her, his Teutonic accent taking on the cadence of a bolero. Their parents had named her Arami because of her bicolor eyes, which he gazed at again and again, as if obsessed....

Even now, María knew she was beautiful. "Filly" they had called her, ever since she had reached puberty: a dark brown filly with black eyes. Standing up straight, she preened in front of the mirror, cinching her waist with her hands and twisting her hips as if she were still a young girl. The manager had had his eye on her from her first day on the job. She thought about the kiss. Old Nazi, dirty old man. "Nazi," she said out loud in the melancholy candor of her ignorance, as if the word were a fragment retrieved from a remote corner of her memory, under a humid, mosquito-heavy sky saturated with the smell of rotten fruit. The manager liked to check her rooms after she finished up. In the bathroom: *Dirty, dirty,* he told her. But nothing was dirty. He just wanted an excuse to come in and look at her and push her up against the marble countertop and empty himself into her body... María knew it was just a ruse, that her bathrooms were impeccably clean, but that little edge in his voice... Nobody was going to teach her how to clean. Nobody. It was an insult, but she put up with it because her job mattered to her. It mattered to her, because it hadn't been easy to get this job in the first place, after so many years of being illegal. It mattered to her, even now, when at last she had her papers and she didn't need to put up with anything anymore; she still put up with it—like Arami might have done?—in spite of her fury at the way the manager sometimes pronounced her name. *Marrriiia,* he called her, with a gargled, strangled "r," and she didn't know if he was making fun of her, or if it was something else.

If you could only hear him, Arami, you'd know what to say to me.

Her fury stemmed from the fact that "María" was her chosen, artistic name. During her years at the cabaret she had changed it from Panambi, the name she was born with. Yes, she was once a showgirl: a *real* showgirl, she reminded herself with a touch of aging panache, not because she had ever feared sex, but because she had considered herself an artist. Since when do whores need to know how to sing? And the fact is she did know how to sing and had been, in her day, as beautiful as María Félix. The same beauty mark, the same eyebrows, she thought, bending her face so close to the mirror that she almost brushed her reflection. The beauty mark didn't look the same on wrinkled skin. María moved her face away from the mirror and tugged at the deep lines on her cheeks. She called herself "María" as in María Félix or Mary Magdalene, not as in the Virgin Mary. Merciful God, the cart was so heavy. In the light of the elevator, she could see herself as she used to appear after singing, in a low-cut gown instead of a uniform, her breasts pushed proudly forward so that anyone could see her heart beating. So that he would see the rapid flutter of her pulse and take her out on the dance floor.

But he never did. Arami was always there ahead of her. Like María, she was one of the most popular girls in the cabaret, but unlike María, she wasn't a singer. Arami was possessed of a furtive, feral nature. She had a baby bird imprisoned inside her, an anxious pair of wings in her bony, fragile chest. She liked to walk barefoot through the fields, embracing the wind. Sky, universe, lightning, misty rain. Arami left the house, lay down on a tall, icy table, and let him inject her, and then it was "Uncle" this and "Uncle" that, every time she opened her mouth. "Wise," she called him, because he had wanted to found a new world, a new order. She bragged that he was going to fix her eyes, so he could leave his seed inside her even better. María felt a shiver pass through her body as she yanked down the hem of her uniform.

It was you who was spiteful, Arami. And bad: quesú. *You left me. You left me all alone.*

María looked up at the bright lights. "The manager is mine," she thought to herself. She remembered one afternoon. "Panambi, let me have him. Fly away like a butterfly, Panambi," her sister had begged her, because it wasn't in Arami's nature to fight. By then they had stopped going to the movies together: Arami had forgotten all about Pedro Infante, Agustín Lara, and even Jorge Negrete, who married María Félix. "*De porá* means *you're handsome,*" Arami said.

Handsome, Arami? Come on! You don't see his huge, ugly hands, his head like a block of wood, his weak jaw and buck teeth, you don't see that he's married, that he doesn't know how to love, that even his own son calls him "Uncle Fritz..."

None of it mattered, as María well knew, because every night, with military precision, Fritz showed up at the cabaret and invited her sister to dance. He spun Arami around the floor, as if she were flying, just the tips of her shoes brushing the ground. María sang for him and he sang for Arami, whispering in her ear, "My darling... " Such a tall man, everyone could see him tilting his head down towards Arami's neck, just so he could hear her say, "You're handsome, *de porá.*" While he had told her, the night before he left, "Your flesh is more than a passing malady, Arami. You belong to me."

Marrriiia: it was the manager's voice, in that horrible accent that drove her to fury... Where was it coming from? She hadn't seen him anywhere. She always made sure that she was completely alone. María peeked her head out of the elevator:

nothing. She put her ear to the intercom: nothing. For an instant she thought that the voice was coming from the shaft wall, but no... *Marrriiia*, she heard again: it was the walkie-talkie she had forgotten in the pocket of her uniform. She responded. He wasn't calling her down to his office. "The bathroom in 205 is dirty," he told her. As María started to push the cart out of the elevator, she looked at herself again. But this time the light had changed. Now it seemed to be the reddish, flickering bulb under which Arami screamed as she birthed a stillborn baby with dead blue eyes. "*Añamenby*, devil's spawn," the midwife said, and María once again saw the blood stains, the tall, icy table, and Arami's exhausted, purple arms..."Cleaning is healing," she told herself, and she scrubbed her sister's skin with the same cloth she had used to wash the baby's body. But it took María a very long time to heal; to smell like new again. To leave her body.

Voi potá, Arami. Sky, universe, lightning, misty rain, she said to herself, over and over, huddled up in the corner of the elevator, her cart blocking the door and the walkie-talkie calling: *Mariiia.*

OPENING NIGHT

I

LOOKING BACK AT WHAT happened, he realized that he could have done something to avoid it. He knew that *Carmen* had always appeared in his life as if perchance, a seemingly meaningless coincidence that ended up changing everything. And wasn't it significant enough that the Teatro Colón had announced the premiere on that particular day: the very day when everything began to change for him? But he didn't see it, not then.

He was always a little strange; or it might be closer to the truth to say that he was singular. At the end of the day, he was just a man who worked at a cleaners, someone who was a bit bewildered by life, even a bit slow, perhaps because his parents were already getting on in years when they brought him into the world. He was passionate about music, which was nothing special, really, when you consider the repetitive, timeworn nature of putting clothes in the machines and taking them out, adding detergent, folding and ironing. Over the course of the workday, with its mechanical, mindless rounds of wash, dry, and steam, music is one more customary element. A classic palliative of the profession.

Not really that strange, either, that the music he loved best was opera—there's something for everyone—or that he liked to turn the volume all the way up. You can't go to the cleaners in Buenos Aires without noticing the speakers dominating the space above the washers and dryers. What was singular was that he found the hum and the heat of the machines to be soothing; they helped him to think. Not to ponder or to philosophize—he hated mental circumlocutions that he couldn't understand. What he liked, plain and simple, was to let his imagination loose. During the long pauses while the machines whirled through spin cycle and permanent press, he acted out the operas as he listened to them, creating ovations, moving the principals from overture to recitative to aria to chorus, on the exquisitely modeled set of a toy theater, an exact replica of the Théâtre National de l'Opéra Comique in Paris that he had inherited at the death of his father.

For him the toy theater was not an object of sentimental value; it was a plaything. His father, once an electrician for the best theaters in Buenos Aires, had found it in a storeroom, forgotten and coated with dust, and taken it home. There, it acquired the sacred quality of a holy relic: because the state of his father's nerves precluded him from touching anything fragile, he laid his hands on it for the first time after coming home from the cemetery to the mournful, empty apartment. It was a detailed model of the Parisian set for the opening night of *Carmen*. As his father told the story, the premiere had been a complete fiasco, and Bizet's death from a heart attack three months later was the tragic result.

He opened the cleaners daily at ten o'clock, but he got there much earlier. Always at eight o'clock, with enough time to check the machines, tidy the shop, and even prepare the pickup bags lined up on the shelves below the counter. A little before nine o'clock, he was free to do what he loved best: to play, as earnestly as a child. He took the toy theater down from its shelf, set it on a square table at the back of the shop, behind the machines, and selected the music for the opera he had in mind that day. After carefully placing the principals on the proscenium, he gave himself over to the pleasure of moving them in turn through their roles as the opera slowly progressed.

Because the theater was only designed to represent *Carmen*, he also spent hours fabricating tiny costumed figures for other favorite operas, punching out the paperboard silhouettes, penciling the graceful folds of their attire, and finally applying careful dabs of paint. These were no crudely sketched paper dolls: each figure dazzled with bright precision, down to the last detail. That was his tribute to his mother, also deceased, who had been a seamstress. He had learned from her that the essence of every role is in the costume, the second skin that suspends our disbelief. For his mother had costumed so many bodies behind the scenes. Bodies now nameless in his recollections, bodies he had never even thought to glance at, except one: a woman's body, voluptuous and nearly naked, a body his mother had fitted countless times and whose transformations he witnessed on opening night: unfurling, ascending in an urgent, passionate voice, enthroned by floodlights and exalted by majestic garments. That body, *her* body, destined to become Carmen, Bizet's crown jewel.

He was no longer a child with chubby cheeks, or at least they were well hidden behind the vigorous beard that suited him well. He understood things better now, and found himself able to cope with loneliness, for his parents remained present in every one of his thoughts. In fact, he almost felt they were still beside him. That "almost," it should be said, sometimes weighed heavy on him, especially when he found himself daydreaming about *her*. More than forty years had gone by and he still shivered when he thought about her laughter, her skirts swirling around her rosy skin as she took on the substance of each role she had to play. Living as he did surrounded by clothes, he considered them to be much more than soiled fabric, and he paid more attention to them than his job required, because clothes are what frame and channel our destiny. Clothes give meaning to the bodies they cover. That's what he believed, knowing all the while what his own clothes—gray, inscrutable, nondescript—said about him.

He liked to make guesses about other people's lives based on what they wore. A black girl got on the bus and sat down, gazing out the window. She wore her hair in a bun wrapped with purple cloth. Long beaded earrings, no makeup. Her neck was bare, unless you counted her prominent collarbone as an embellishment. Her purple caftan had long embroidered sleeves and lilac trim around the collar. The hood of the dress, thrown back, revealed her skin and the hint of an elegant, muscular back. She wore leather flats and white pantyhose, clinging to the thick contours of ankles accustomed to work. She must be a dancer, he said to himself, and when he watched her willowy descent from the bus, he knew he had guessed right.

There was nothing too exciting about his life, this man who spent his days working at the cleaners, who was a bit slow, who loved music, and whose unexceptional existence resembled nothing so much as a moth's, emerging at dusk with tiny, brown, battered wings. That's how he felt about himself every night at eight o'clock when he locked up, turned right and walked three blocks along Tucumán, crossed the street, walked through the center of the plaza, then onto the sidewalk, and arrived at the grand entrance of his father's opera house: that is, the Teatro Colón. So many times, as a child and adolescent, he had come with his parents to this house of floodlights and thick cables, always watching from behind the scenes, never out in front in a seat of his own. He wasn't upset about what he had missed, he only unfolded the memories that he had. The brilliantly illuminated chandelier was not part of his memories, nor was the sight of the curtains drawing back to reveal the stage. Yes, that's what occupied his mind during the scant two minutes it took for him to cross the street and leave the Teatro Colón behind, on the way to his apartment.

II

One afternoon a woman walked into the cleaners. She wore a maid's uniform; she had short hair and beautiful hands. She placed on the counter a large oval box, lined with black satin, a box that would set a singular chain of events in motion. He opened it carefully and unfolded a full-dress tailcoat, heavy with the scent of naphthalene. The woman asked him for a receipt itemizing the six articles inside the box, including a top hat, stained along the band and smelling of mildew. He considered the job carefully, estimating both the cost and the likelihood that his efforts might not succeed. "I'll see what we can do. Leave it with me, I'll call you," he said, like his father had taught him, and the maid shrugged, not seeming to care. It was the most interesting job that had come his way in years. He couldn't recall anything quite like it. He had restored evening dresses thick with embroidery and fine lace, had worked on organza, silk shantung, chiffon, linen... Every now and again a lackluster tuxedo, but never—never in life!—a tailcoat like this.

He waited until he was alone to examine it. First he held up the black coat, checking for missing buttons and looking for signs of mildew. He sighed with relief when he saw that although the white silk pocket handkerchief would need to be bleached, the tails themselves, lined with white satin, were spotless. The flat-front trousers perfectly matched the coat, with a dark satin stripe running down the outside of each leg. Then there was the moiré silk waistcoat, once pearl gray but now yellowing along the seams. The white dress shirt, of fine cotton, had French cuffs and a high collar. He thought that with heavy starch, the collar and shirt front would come out as good as new. Last but not least, from a tiny plastic bag he retrieved the bow tie, in better condition than the waistcoat. It was perfect. As he looked over the ensemble, he felt that he was experiencing an epiphany.

That night he brought the box home with him, wanting to start right away. He walked three blocks down Tucumán, crossed the street, walked through the plaza. At these hours he enjoyed the plaza more, empty as it was of the stray dogs that terrorized it every morning. No barking now, no honking horns, just human shadows coming and going, slower than they did in the daytime, as if they were paperboard silhouettes, ready to be painted. Lights shone on all four sides of the opera house. A show was going on; he saw the posters. He arrived at the grand entrance, circled around to the marquee on the right side of the building, and read the letters slowly: "Car... men." An exceptional coincidence. He thought of the gypsy, the jealous lover, and the toreador from his theater. Still, he didn't linger long in front of the marquee. He didn't know that the sigh that escaped his lips signified something more than resignation: it was the unresolved yearning of his heart, unexpectedly sparked and just as quickly destined to be extinguished. A cleaner's life is too narrow and pale to nurture that kind of fluttering.

But later, sitting at his mother's sewing table, under the light of the same lamp that his father had installed for her years ago, with the theme from *Carmen* reverberating privately in his eardrums, he made the extraordinary vow to return. Only this time he wouldn't hang back in the shadows. And his parents, wherever they were now, would be proud of him. They wouldn't feel sad anymore about his occasional loneliness. He made the decision almost in defiance of himself, moved by the memory of the thousands of times he had been paralyzed by fear: that *she* would be there, would reject him, and that the inertia that until now had protected him would prove fatal. It was better to not let suffering in; his parents had this made clear, and he had done their bidding, without entirely letting go of the illusions brought to life by the question "What if...?"

Truthfully, though, he wasn't thinking in terms of future possibilities. What occupied his mind was a single instant, the moment of their encounter. He'd see her again. He would be waiting for her when the show ended, holding out a single red carnation and, perhaps—could he even conceive of such a perhaps?—he would kiss her as passionately as she had that day, pressing him backwards into the heavy rows of costumes, gracing him with the first and only kiss of his life. Good God, how his mother had raged at her when she found them together. Bad words had poured out of her mouth and he had listened from the safety of the dressing room next door, helpless to stop her. Wails. Sobs. A slammed door. And the word "pity" like a stinging blow, following him all the way home to his dull and silent room.

III

Time went by quickly, and so did his work restoring the

tailcoat. So absorbing was the task that he lost interest in playing with the toy theater, which sat on its shelf, carelessly pushed back. To the rhythm of his favorite arias, his thoughts were flurries of possible outcomes and words. He wrote them down in his black spiral notepad and then made revisions, like his father had taught him. He had crossed out the word "Hello," and then many others. At last he decided on silence. "Let her be the first to speak." He would give her a moment to recognize him, standing there by himself, mature and stylish with his impeccable beard. All by himself, without anyone else to support him: as an adult. Seeing himself as an adult gave him an exciting sense of his own strength, which augmented every time he tried on part of the suit. The moiré waistcoat fitted him perfectly, and the trouser hems just brushed his shoes. As he put on the coat, a marvelous transformation overtook him; even the tone of his voice changed.

Opening night was only one day away—not even a day, just a matter of hours!—and he hadn't experienced a single moment of remorse. His parents had always encouraged him to spend money on himself. Without hesitation, he paid a small fortune for the best orchestra seat available, then splurged on new socks and black dress shoes. It comforted him to do his parents' bidding, one last time. He had everything. Everything but the red carnation, which he planned to pick up from the florist's stall on the corner of Tucumán, on the way to the opera house. He had paid for it in advance, after crossing the plaza that morning, just to be sure. He closed up for lunch, something he never did, and walked to his father's favorite barbershop, where they cut his hair and trimmed his beard the way his mother had liked best. Then he went back to the shop, where he planned to leisurely iron the suit. He didn't eat, because he wasn't hungry.

Carmen played loudly on the speakers all afternoon. He

sang along as he pressed each article of his elegant suit. First he pressed all the white pieces, and then the dark ones. He spritzed them with a bit of cologne, like his mother used to do, and carefully laid them one by one on the counter to air out. He closed his eyes and listened for a moment to the peaceful sound of the machines, moving in sync with his heartbeat, which pulsed in his chest, his throat, and even his knees, with a fervor he had never felt before. He wasn't a moth anymore. He would go to the opera with butterfly wings. Even a cleaner can be a king if he truly wishes. The meaning of his father's saying opened to him, like a flower that only blooms in the sunlight. At eleven o'clock, when touched by a ray of light, it reveals itself. He could be a king, he could be anything he wished. It was hard waiting to get dressed. If it had been up to him, he would have changed at three o'clock, right after coming back from the barbershop. He longed to do it now, to walk the streets of the city until showtime. But he didn't want to be all sweaty when he arrived at the opera house. No. It was a bad idea.

That's what he was thinking when he heard the little bell his mother had tied to the door so that he would know when someone walked into the shop. He looked at the clock with large numbers that his father had placed on the wall. It was a quarter past six. Everything happened so fast. The second hand ticked only once as he felt the impulse to run and lock the door, to push whoever was there out onto the street. But his feet stayed put. At the door was the woman in the maid's uniform, the one with short hair and beautiful hands.

"You did it!" she said, as she held up the coat from the counter. "It's incredible! You're an artist!"

He thought about lying so he wouldn't have to return the suit. "It's not ready yet" was all he would have to tell her. But she pressed forward into the shop as he turned down the music.

"I just figured I'd stop by to see how things were going," she explained, almost apologizing. "You didn't call, so we wondered... But never mind! Would you pack it back up in the box for me?"

He hadn't called her. How could he have forgotten? His mother would never have let this happen. It was for exactly this reason that his father had given him his spiral notepad. While he mechanically folded the flat-front trousers with their satin stripes, the woman counted the articles that lay on the counter.

"And the bow tie and hat make six. Perfect!" She beamed. Without a murmur, she paid the agreed-upon sum and told him to keep the change.

The little bell chimed again, breaking the spell that should have already been broken by his premonition. It was seven o'clock, exactly when he had planned to begin getting dressed. He would have started with the socks, then the trousers... At that moment, the shop seemed to him like a cemetery. He walked back and forth among the silent machines and the baskets of clothes. The light turned the walls an oppressive yellow. The stillness overwhelmed him. A line of cars passed slowly on the other side of the glass door, like in a silent film. His pupils held the afterimage of the blinking red lights. Shouts of *Carmen* issued from the speakers and echoed throughout the shop, but without penetrating his ears. He walked in smaller and smaller circles, finally arriving at the table in the back, as dizzy and bewildered as a child. He took his toy theater down from the shelf and set it carefully on the table, where he could think of nothing else to do except play, for a very long time, before returning at last to his strange, or rather, his singular life.

VERTICAL DREAM

SHE DREAMED THAT she was fast asleep—just like when she was a child, carried away by the flow of her mother's voice and the stories she told, or resting her head on her father's chest as he rocked her with his smoker's wheezing breath. Back then it had been a relief to close her eyes and sleep a little, despite her excitement and everything she had to learn and remember, like all those numbers and directions, like the weight of her guilt as her freedom unfolded. It couldn't exactly be said, however, that she'd had trouble falling asleep on the eve of the big day. She'd spent a long time half-awake, looking out her window, the faraway, shaky lights of the city killing her slowly.

"Are you asleep?" Her father opened the bedroom door slightly, and a yellow triangle of light filtered through, illuminating the floor. She didn't answer, although she did hear him. She didn't want to have to lie: to talk over, once again, the itinerary, the streets, the buses, the address of the Scottish professor in charge of meeting students whose cosmic luck led them to the dorms, their future confirmed, approved. As her departure loomed, it became more and more difficult for her to keep track of the hours. Her father looked at her, full of pride, for once sparing her the weight of his expectations, as if already reaping the fruits of some task carried to completion. He was vulnerable and on the verge of tears, and for this reason, she closed her eyes, pretending to be sleeping, her back to the big window.

Her window was one in an infinite wall of windows, stacked atop one another like framed paintings that revealed the secrets of their subjects. In front and on both sides, at an unimpressive distance, stood similar walls and they encouraged voyeurism: everyone there liked being watched. The windows, scrupulously cleaned, awaited the nightly pornography; in the daytime, they remained uninhabited, empty. They glowed with artificial, amber lights that bathed each interior with brittle luster, gave epic proportions to the daily minutiae: ordinary events became tall tales, some with more art (more realism) than others, depending on the talent and lineage of their performers. For example, an evening meal became an epicurean feast, glorifying the simple biological function that was swallowing. Life's fantasies on display in every window. And as for her, they'd taught her to be wary of any kind of exposure, so that she couldn't imagine herself being looked at. She could barely look at herself in the mirror. Although, sometimes, in secret, she did.

Nothing portrayed in the windows was ugly—nothing abject, nothing miserable. And this, precisely—the mindlessness, the vanity—attracted her. The tenants of these windows were never crude or unrefined, not even when the living painting focused on tragedy—for example, a death—because these dark episodes were also an artistic representation of the world, an imitation achieved with meticulous skill, designed to please. Aren't heroic events, however small, predestined for glory?

Objects mattered, even in their economy. Few, but beautiful. Few, but significant. Few, but never excessively fine: a cordovan lounger; a couple of books, bound in leather like fetishes, left on a table; a green desk lamp; or one of these new ergonomically designed gadgets, the kind that produce perfectly aromatic Sumatran coffee without bruising a single grain.

She had believed that everything was judiciously lit to arouse admiration or idolatry, although the compliments were easy, the kisses vain, and the affections insincere. And also, the warmth of simply being, it's well known, tends to acclimate, numb, and finally bore you... But it was illogical, wasn't it? That so much time could be spent composing these small evening tableaus, when so few people walked by: just a few moments at night, after hours of work during which one had run endlessly so that something memorable could be created after dark. Forget the present, forget the now. People carried around an obsession with the future—a fear. It disturbed them—like a nightmare unfolding—the idea that they, or their successors, might descend into vulgarity, or worse, poverty. For poverty was the quintessence of horror. The windows were not only a form of vain ostentation, but also a connection with the world they yearned for, and a defensive barrier against the world they feared.

Her window (all the windows of her house, in fact) was an exception on that wall. A picture window with curtains that were thin, but not transparent. She lived there with her family in a pristine environment, unsoiled, almost sacred. They had little furniture, numerous books—so many stacks that they no longer fit anywhere—and an old grand piano. Neither she nor her younger brother had ever gone to school; their parents saw to that. Teachers by trade, they homeschooled their children to shield them from the obscenity of this other world that they rejected for its posturing, its indifference to what they believed to be true. They valued courage, honesty and intelligence. They were "enlightened," determined to instill knowledge in their children so that all doors would open to them. They discussed methods and content, the evolution of literature and language. Science, art, but also the care of body and soul. Their father taught the past, attempting a dialogue with history; he kept faith with the classics and ancient languages, establishing the primacy of Latin, along with other indispensable tongues. Their mother, on the other hand, celebrated the present and prepared her children for the future, focusing on science in all its practical applications. Films and music also helped them to mold the souls of their warriors. The girl played the piano with a frightening innate virtuosity. Her brother, the violin. At some point they had to learn to shield themselves from the mockery of the other children who roamed the outside world, until they felt capable of presenting themselves to others, much like vegetarians who refuse to eat meat without embarrassment. They acquired, as a defense mechanism, an astute sense of humor they used to sidestep their critics.

Their parents not only showed them the beauty of the world, they also taught them about what they saw as the dire reality of its shortcomings. That false world to which they didn't belong—even when they believed otherwise—and instead of which they had chosen a monasticism that isolated the family over time, turning the children into laboratory specimens that their parents meant to fix, enhance, refine with the chisel of their beliefs.

Sometimes, because of the children's curiosity (mostly hers), the parents opened the curtains for educational and comparative purposes. Over the years, she'd secretly drawn back these curtains herself and looked out the window. She wondered about the reality of both worlds, and of others that she might not even know about. Increasingly she felt as if she were an encrypted message that no one cared to decipher. Often she sought pleasure, gripped by the pure desire to enjoy, but she always fell back into the austerity of her family. She thought over and over about her gifts as a burden, asking herself whether intelligence and erudition could lead to arrogance and boasting. She wondered if courage and honesty were not also cruel forms of labeling everything, so that one could pretend to be better than the rest. She did not know which route to follow on the family map. But she craved an emergency exit: she wanted to escape, breathe: be brought to life: cut the wires carefully woven over the years. To flee from the ancient and venerable university, founded in the fifteenth century in the priory of a cathedral. To abandon the obsequious precision of mathematics and music; to rip off the corset. "Give me the superfluous; for anybody can have the necessary." She'd repeated this secret war cry ever since adolescence. At those times, words completely lost their meaning, as if in her memory, the parts of an infinite puzzle had been scattered.

She felt rage, but also pity for her parents. She thought about everything she had been taught, and about the futility of knowledge. Can a creation betray its creator without being punished? Can a work of art aspire to be anything but what has been dreamed by the artist? She pondered these questions the night before her departure, in the solitude of her room, looking out at the windows that resembled paintings.

She rose from her bed, walked to her own window, and peered down at the street below. On the sidewalk a woman cowered, her feet bare against the pavement. Beside her, discreetly, lay a stiff human form. She imagined the woman was crying from the cold, because that's what people cry over, the ones who are going nowhere: the cold... They were protecting themselves not only from the wind, but also the light, which revealed everything with its patina: the trash heaps and the dead-end roads; the dogs, street corners, and windows. The road stretching towards the unknown was made of fear; the world's glory lay on the other side of misery. Just now, the moonlight was beginning to wane. The girl also felt the cold, like a premonition, but did not stop looking out. Fast asleep, or maybe not at all sleeping, she simply looked out the window.

MOEBIA

*The certainty that everything has already been written
annuls us, or renders us phantasmal.*

JORGE LUIS BORGES (TRANS. ANDREW HURLEY)

THE NIGHT HAD BEEN long, and the prison was silent with
the breath of revenge, or at least that's what the warden chose
to believe; otherwise, nothing made sense. The sight left him
speechless: your man half-naked, with his trousers at his knees,
mouth open and drooling, maybe wasted, maybe on a bad
trip—a dirty slump on the mat. The baby lay next to him, her
legs open, bent, and limp, like a broken doll. Dead.

Yes, Magdalena: this time, the one they called "your
man" woke up in Hell, the prison guards kicking him as
he tried to process the reason for the shouts around him.
Small, sharp needles of light forced him back into reality,
as his eyes adjusted slowly. He was struggling to sit up when

he saw them taking your daughter's body away, covered up by a blanket. Still on his knees, he tried to get to her but fell face down on the floor in a faint. When he opened his eyes again, he later told you, he found himself in a green, dimly lit room; he could smell that someone was smoking cigarettes very close to him. His nose and forehead were swollen like a dry cork, still throbbing. "I didn't do it, I swear!" he sobbed, and those words would remain his only defense.

No. Let's not call you naive, Magdalena. For in naiveté, there is innocence and bewilderment. You were never innocent. If it makes you feel better, you can say that, in your eyes, Moebia had ceased to be the embodiment of horror, depravation, and putrescence. In your eyes, Moebia was no longer a prison, but simply an archaic structure, a labyrinthine palace with, oh, so many towers! And, oh, so many rooms! Like an adobe hive. That place allowed you to live in the most improbable kind of parallel universe, with no present, no future, among all the different languages and all the different kinds of inmates: men, women, and children mixing promiscuously in this serpentarium. You convinced yourself that none of it was real, that none of it was serious, and that what mattered was that you had good reasons. Important reasons: your little girl, of course, and also Rafael... Well, keep telling yourself whatever you want. Keep running in circles.

Ghosts surround you. Time usually soothes dark memories—but not yours: you are not yet ready to forget. You'd have to let go of him, Magdalena. And what would remain then? At least, you know that Rafael never lied to you, that he never had it in him to deceive you, that he always showed his true colors. In this world, few men are so unashamed, so impudent. Even when they caught him working as a mule, with thirty balloons in his gut, he was defiant. They convicted him, and he'd almost served his three years in Moebia when what happened... happened. But, for him, Moebia had never meant condemnation, but rather predestination. He was blond and well mannered, so everybody liked him, and El Pata was enraptured. Rafael had charisma, an innate and limitless ability to seduce, thanks to which his incarceration soon became bearable, almost easy. From the moment he arrived in prison, people noticed him: he stood out among the masses, with the long golden curls that reached his shoulders, his firm chest, and the flicker in his perpetually amused eyes. His gestures were never vulgar, but also never effeminate. Yes, he stood out, there was no one he didn't attract, and this made him the perfect vehicle to transport and carry, to come and go, to give and receive.

El Pata, on the other hand, was a small man, his jaw scarred by a dagger's blade at the age of thirteen. He understood that the drug trade was the ministry of fascination. He had a method. First: enticement. And later: slavery. You'd watched him. He chose his prey and played with it for a day or two. He anointed his followers with all kinds of privileges: banquets, gypsy dances... The prison guards knew to stay away from El Pata's men. But, above all, he gave them a fragile sense of trust, self-respect, and filial protection, all of which was reinforced with increasingly savage initiation rites. In this way, they were reduced to submission; ears were cut and bodies brutally raped. And then, they were reduced to oblivion; he took away everything, but continued to issue commands and punish them, until finally they rejoined the inner circle.

But Rafael was special. El Pata was under a trance, just like you. So you must acknowledge that, in this sense, you two were no different. You imagined the start of it all: Rafael in the tight jeans he always wore to show off his big package. Reptilian eyes undressed him, lingering on the round ass hugged by thin cloth, as the man feverishly envisioned fucking him... The others told you the rest: El Pata approached him openly, offering his protection and taking him under his wing. That very night, El Pata rode him like a climbing plant, but also howled as he was penetrated by Rafael, dominated by his strength, made helpless by his beauty. Your man was aware of his telluric magnetism. He walked around like he owned the place. Most of the time he slept with El Pata, but he sometimes screwed a guard or some other prisoner's wife. El Pata allowed it.... Why was it so difficult for you to understand his nature?

By now, the time for tragedy and disbelief has passed. Time hierarchizes the intensity of pain. Do you think about this as you brush your pearly white teeth, from top to bottom, and then from bottom to top, 1-2-3 times on one side and then on the other, first the outer surfaces, and then the ones that are harder for the brush to reach? How much did your arrogance have to do with it, Magdalena? Do you think about that? You arrived on a gray day. You wanted to bring down the ones in charge. For you, journalism was a type of moral despotism, which you practiced by trusting your nose for front-page stories. And the hunger for attention is insatiable. You were willing to use all your might and all your influence to get the scoop. You knew yourself well. There was something both repulsive and appealing about you. Something offensive and somewhat disquieting. It had to do with your intelligence, the way you dug up dirt, the way you asked all the right questions. What were you aspiring to? More glory? Don't lie, Magdalena. You weren't looking for trophies; you had them all. You wanted more than admiration. Your barren heart craved affection; you just wanted to be loved. But who could love you, Magdalena? Sometimes, you couldn't even come to love yourself. Rumor had it that you hated other women, but this was not true; you simply despised beauty. You'd learned that defense mechanism during childhood: you held a cloak of disdain over whatever you weren't good at. And you were not just imperfect, Magdalena. You were plain ugly, plain hideous, grotesque even, and it led to your solitude. You spent hours immolating your body and hardening your heart. Your public face—resolute and imperturbable—only accentuated your hauteur.

The doors of Moebia opened for you. Such is the omnipotence of fear. You were persistent and you almost succeeded in getting what you were looking for. *Almost.* You believed that you could alter the course of events, having always done so before. Not this time. I'll give you credit, though: anyone could make an accusation, but only you were willing to write the story. The long lines on visiting days were not made up of relatives, but rather pilgrims who came from all over the world to visit the famous "cocaine prison." That was the scoop!

You lied about your reasons for coming. Let's say it without euphemisms: you were deceitful. But when did you ever care about procedures? One afternoon, you decided to find El Pata and write a story that would blow up his mythology. You announced it petulantly to the newsroom staff: "If you strip the symbolic trappings from the heroes, you get to the flesh." Your plan was to walk in and meet him, but Rafael stopped you. The click of your boots down the corridor woke him from his siesta, but he pretended to be asleep, stretched out in his hammock, blocking your way. I bet you stared at him, traced his hard abdomen with your eyes, and imagined unzipping his already half-open fly. But the truth is that when he opened his eyes to surprise you, you looked down.

"I came to talk to him," you said, sure he would know who you were referring to.

"Why don't you talk to me?" he answered with a smile. "I can tell you whatever you want to know."

"I'm not interested," you replied.

Your heart skipped and your brain buzzed. Never before had you met a man of that caliber, who, to top it all, was giving you the time of day. Ugly women know that men don't look at them, least of all men like Rafael, because the world is obsessed with perfect proportions: beauty over brain, shine over substance. You had studied these facts to erudition. From the beginning of times, from Aristotle to Nietzsche, beauty was the territory of contemplation and goodness, while ugliness was the space of repulsion and violence, much worse than no place at all. You wished ugliness could have been simply the opposite of beauty: a symmetrical counterpoint. But it was worse than that; it brought out the most human, and therefore the most perverse reactions—disgust, hate, and terror. That's why you saw Frankenstein as the most sincere parable of humanity: the monster fleeing to his death. Beauty shook people and made them stupid, but you had never before experienced its impact, its frenzy, and its paralysis. If love at first sight exists, it must be a drug like this one: poisonous. You didn't want to see him again because you felt him in your veins as an addiction, and you knew you would be unable to free yourself. So, of course, you came back every day. Even then you pretended you didn't know him for who he was, even then you mocked him. You were cruel. Rafael liked your black humor and the strange circumstance that you were immune to his charms. He waited eagerly for your arrival; he followed you around the prison and laid siege to your life outside, sending you gifts made with his own hands and calling you on the phone.

You kept coming, Magdalena—not for the paper, but for him. First, for a coffee hour. Then, for an afternoon. And then, for an entire night. It was not just about Rafael, but also about the way you felt there. In prison you were learning another sense of beauty, one you had read about, but that you had invariably mocked. Something immaterial and innocent, something you had to come back for because it brought you joy and even peace. You imagined prison as an artistic representation of the world, that is to say, ugliness masterfully imitated, which acquires a beautiful resonance. Your time there was beautiful in that way, for you felt yourself freed, welcomed, and not in the sense of sententious admiration, not as if you were a pearl among swine, but because you were a part of the whole. You laughed at yourself, for you could feel the dislocation in your soul caused by this rapturous and unhealthy tenderness. El Pata saw you from afar and understood how you fit into that mess. He threatened Rafael, warned him of the dangers, but it was useless. Then he confronted you, without any effect. You refused to listen and you ended up living with Rafael in prison. You moved into a prison, Magdalena! You paid to spend the night and you left in the morning.

When you were kicked out of the paper, you didn't care. You would write a book—you swore it—a true work of art, with which you would touch the sun at its zenith. You manipulated events as easily as if you were cheating at cards, and this gave you a sense of scientific authority, since you were proving your theory that destiny was, in fact, subject to appeal. Rafael was serving the last of his sentence and, although you didn't plan it, it happened that he made you pregnant. You had rejected the archetype of motherhood at a young age, but now you embraced it easily, as one more aspect of your existential metamorphosis. Then the girl was born and El Pata, in exchange for leaving father and daughter alone, demanded that Rafael's visits to him continue. They spent nights together, in spite of Rafael's anxiety to be with you. He returned every morning like an exile; you solemnized his homecoming as your revenge and personal triumph. El Pata felt that he'd been tricked, so why wouldn't he seek vengeance? By taking your daughter's life, he thought he could take what he really wanted.

Rafael explained these facts so insistently that the warden interceded and sent samples of his DNA out of the country for testing. But they also listened to him because of your own influence, Magdalena. Mutilated by your daughter's death, you roared for justice, watching your architecture fall to pieces around you. All you wanted was to go back to prison because you had been happy there to the point of insensibility; you wanted to return to that refuge where everything was so dead that even your thorns didn't show. What made you think it was possible to achieve happiness? Why did you dare to imagine a life with him on the outside? Why did you betray your own faith and surrender to the delirium of perfection? Now you were defeated by the certainty that you were losing everything. You had no strength left, Magdalena. You felt besieged by the inaccuracy of the facts, by the severity of your own judgment and the blind rage in your heart. Your man drifted in a catatonic sleep, far away from you. He just lay there. Did he blame you? Had he stopped loving you? Did he reproach you for your doubts? For the first time, Magdalena, the pull of what others said was stronger. You had awakened. The press poured out the fury of their ink as they awaited the results of the DNA test, fateful results that arrived on the Friday morning when Rafael was found dead in his cell. You made yourself believe that your hands were clean. You hid what you knew; you made the results of the lab tests disappear, because your mission in life was always narcissistic. Then you just got back to writing your book. Get as high as the sun and burn.

GOURMET

THERE WAS A place she would have liked to return to. It was a bedroom in her grandparents' house, a room her grandmother had decorated especially for her, even though at first the fabrics and the colors seemed a bit too grown up. Abuela had stitched the comforter herself, along with the curtains and the bed cushions, so that they would last a lifetime. Hence, Inés's taste for checkered bedspreads: it all originated from that first, fluffy comforter, white and blue, with checks on one side and flowers on the other. After dinner, Abuela would prepare the bed for her to sleep in. She would spread out the comforter and then turn it down, revealing just the tops of the pillows in their white, embroidered pillowcases. On the bedside table, the lit lamp, a small pitcher of water and a glass, a box of tissues, and a book, usually one of Abuela's recommendations. There was also the scent of lavender, which rose softly from the corners of the room, because of a few fresh sprigs or a candle left by her grandmother. In that room, Abuela could cure her of anything. When Inés was a teenager, Abuela would lead her by the hand to the room, tuck her into bed, remove the cushions, and pull the curtains until the room became night. In the warmth of the closed room, Abuela would sit beside her, combing her hair until she was deeply asleep. Because sleep is the best of all cures, her grandmother said, and Inés believed it, heart and soul.

So whenever she needed something to help her cope, Inés lay in the dark, on her bed, wherever that bed might be: Buenos Aires, Oslo, Abidjan... She closed her eyes and tried to conjure up a pleasant aroma—if not lavender, let's say cinnamon—to allow her to purge whatever daylight in each new country could not suppress. On that summer afternoon in the Amazon, not long after Manuel's most recent relocation, the tension was high, so Inés threw herself face down on her fluffy comforter. When she woke up, hours later, she felt almost wholesome, as if propelled by the force of twilight: "We have to make friends!" she said. It sounded so childish that Manuel started laughing. But she insisted, like a breathless puppy. "I need to talk to other people. I feel so alone." He sensed that if he did not agree, her strange euphoria would soon turn into tears. So he encouraged her to invite people over. "But who?" she asked, pouting with pessimism. "People from the school," he answered automatically, without even thinking. Inés remained pensive for a while, and then began to tally up the children who occasionally came to their house and the parents she met at dismissal. In the end, it wasn't too hard to make a list and move on to the menu.

What would she make? Certainly nothing too fussy, too eager to please; something universal that would agree with everyone's taste. Inés called the women, set a date for next week, and started the preparations. Occasionally, Manuel chimed in: "What about pork?" (because he loved pork). "Too heavy," she said. "Fish, maybe?" he offered—just to say something, really, since he didn't even like fish. And she decided that fish was perfect. She went to the market very early in the morning to get a mammoth twenty-pounder, which she cooked slowly in the oven, generously bathed in lemon, garlic and parsley, wrapped in aluminum foil to allow the juices to mix with the butter. Inés didn't care that it had been windy since dawn, with heavy rain all afternoon. She knew herself; she knew that any tremor in her spirit could make her want to die, but only after killing Manuel first. So she would serve—yes, oh, yes—her big fish with sweet potatoes and green bell peppers, both liberally seasoned with lemon. "And why not an appetizer?" she improvised, lit up with the fires of inspiration. Something delicate, from the only cookbook she owned. She flew back to the market. Soon she was mixing plain mayonnaise with minced celery and parsley, spicy pickled peppers, mustard, and a few drops each of Worcestershire sauce and Tabasco. She then cleaned and cut the crabmeat, and soaked several avocado halves in lemon juice. Finally she laid a bed of watercress on each plate, added a halved avocado, stuffed it with crabmeat, and topped everything with a lavish spoonful of sauce. For a garnish, she added chopped tomatoes and black olives. Manuel watched, astonished by her newly acquired culinary skills. "Everything has lemon!" he said, looking out the window, where the rain poured down harder than ever. Inés turned toward him, embattled, furious at his comment, but found herself facing an exhausted man. She realized that she was not the only one who felt uprooted, floating in this new, hellish city. "Let's set the table," she said.

These were the scenes from her life that Inés wished she could assemble into a collage to preserve them forever, even if they were more than a little staged: she and Manuel potting plants and choosing the best places for them in the new house; or the two of them eating orange sherbet from the same bowl while looking at photos of a happier time together. Now they were getting ready to bring the dishes to the table, him singing like Charles Aznavour, and her pretending to be happy. Inés wondered if Manuel also cried, although she preferred to believe the old adage that men don't cry. It was her way of balancing the scales: in truth, Manuel had always loved her more than she loved him, and until lately, he had never seemed to consider this a disadvantage.

Manuel looked at the time. They had invited their guests for eight o'clock, and it was now past nine. Inés hurried in and out of the kitchen, wrapped in a cloud of garlic and butter. She circled the table nervously, placing a candle here, a napkin there, asking Manuel to get changed quickly, but first to cut the bread. Outside there was thunder. Manuel stood with his back to the kitchen, covering his digital watch with his hand to stop himself from looking at it again. He thought about stepping out for a bit, so he wouldn't have to face Inés when she started asking what time it was. In their country, arriving thirty minutes late was reasonable, but to be an hour late was a very bad sign. He was sweaty, even after his shower, and he heard the seconds ticking away in his chest. He understood what awaited him, the storm of her anger pounding him against the rocks: his job, his never having wanted children, their years of exile... Inés would cry, and she would hate him until he begged her forgiveness, a little of which she would grant every day, leaving signs of peace strewn throughout the house. He knew the ritual well, only this time he felt too exhausted to follow it. If no one came to the party, Inés would sink first, and then she would sink him into a swamp of reproaches, suffocating Manuel as surely as the smell of fermented fruit, heavy on the ground of that tree-infested city. Again: a flash of lightning outside the window. Inés had also gotten changed. Her face was washed, she wore just a touch of lipstick, her eyes were serene—or perhaps she had been crying, Manuel thought, as he followed her in silence to the kitchen.

It was almost ten o'clock when the bell rang, surprising Manuel, who stood motionless by the door. Inés smiled, beckoning him to open it. She looked lovely now, like a wide-eyed girl about to attend her first party. He smiled at her as he walked to the door. He greeted the guests, who had arrived en masse, leading them into the living room. The guests had brought wine. He thanked them. He didn't know what to say about the bottles because he had no idea what was what. Wine gave Manuel acid reflux and was too bitter for his taste; he could only tolerate it occasionally. He chose to talk about the weather instead, about the torrential rains, until his wife came to his rescue. She introduced herself casually, lit the candle she had placed on the side table, and very soon took over the conversation, laughing at herself, at her dubious cooking skills and her new kitchen arsenal, warning them about the unpredictable outcome of her culinary experiments. Manuel had always admired this in Inés, her ability to secure the affection of others by disarming them with her vulnerability, her unscripted approach to life: traits that were somehow infallibly attractive. He looked at her and breathed more easily. They had dodged the bullet. At least for tonight.

A REAL MIRACLE

CATALINA SKIPPED through the house preparing for her trip to the countryside. She was thrilled because, for the first time, her father was allowing her to go, even though she'd be gone for many days, they'd be traveling by bus, and Alejandra hit her sometimes—all reasons Papa could have used to say no. Papa didn't like Alejandra. In fact, when she wasn't within earshot, he referred to her as "that little bitch." Mama, on the other hand, had liked Alejandra because she was the daughter of her neighbor, who was also Mama's childhood friend and whom Catalina called Auntie, even though she wasn't her aunt at all. And, of course, since every one of Mama's wishes had become sacred after her death, Papa had agreed to let Catalina go. She was starting to believe in miracles. Miracles bathed in pity, not produced by any saint, but rather by her gleaming orphaned face. Catalina knew—because her mother had explained it to her many times—that you can't please everyone all the time, and you shouldn't get angry about it. She also knew that when adults called someone "naughty," they actually meant "unbearable." She wondered with religious curiosity if the people who now treated her so kindly were not simply faking it because they feared that her mother might be spying on them from the heavens. There was no other way to explain the transformation of Mrs. Isadora, for example, who was as horrible as a fat pigeon, and who always used to make Catalina eat green bean salad when she knew she hated it; and now suddenly she was always asking, "And what can I get for the little lady?"

Oh! If Papa only knew: what she liked about Alejandra wasn't playing with her. She liked her family's apartment; she liked pretending to be part of that family. There was no need to tell this to Papa. He'd feel bad about it and, besides, he wouldn't understand what it was that Catalina liked about the noise, the mess, and the way Alejandra's siblings interrupted one another and snatched things away from each other. She liked their loud laughter, and the way it never seemed to echo. In Catalina's house, everything echoed, especially Papa's footsteps. Catalina listened to them as he got out of the elevator, came down the hall, and opened the heavy security door to their apartment. That was something else she liked about Alejandra's house: there were no bars on the door because they had a dog, a black dog with a loud bark. Papa had put up the bars because of the recent kidnappings, and the robbers who would come into your house and put a gun to your head and take everything. They could very well shoot you and kill the dog, too... Poor Papa.

But Catalina wanted to think only of the trip. To forget about the empty little bottles of whiskey she discovered hidden under the cushions of the easy chair. She wanted only to think about what they would sing on the bus, because Auntie had a nice voice, just like Mama's, and she sang with the girls using different voices as if she were a one-woman choir. Catalina liked to sing, but not as much as she liked cooking. She was so excited that she had prepared a bag of sandwiches for the road, like Mama used to, with hard-boiled eggs and mayonnaise. Papa explained that these sandwiches were good enough to eat at home, but that there was nothing more repulsive than egg salad and the fart-like smell that would impregnate the bus when she opened the bag. But Catalina paid him no mind, because not taking the sandwiches would have been a betrayal of her mother. Papa, giving in at last, tucked her plush blanket into the top of her backpack, along with a bag full of sweets and potato chips to share with the other girls, which he hoped would make his daughter forget all about the sandwiches.

Catalina rang the doorbell three times in a row. Papa had to take her hand away from the button. The door opened and a voice shouted, "Come on in." The girl's heart almost came out of her mouth when she saw all the bundles scattered in the hall. She looked at the baskets of food, the clothes overflowing from the badly closed suitcases, and the toys packed in plastic shopping bags. There was too much of everything, shoved in every which way. Papa worried about how in the world all of this was supposed to fit on the bus, and he fretted that it would make them late. But Auntie said, "No worries, we've got time."

That was just like Auntie. Papa might change his mind. He didn't understand how Auntie could be late to everything, brush her girls' hair in the elevator in front of whoever happened to be there, or invite people over for dinner, only to start cooking after the guests arrived. Mama, on the other hand, had wished she could have been a little more like Auntie. Freer, she used to say, and so Catalina watched Auntie carefully, trying to emulate her. Papa was irritated by Catalina's recent absent-mindedness. Still, she copied Auntie's ways eagerly, leaving her thermos every day in the school bathroom. This infuriated Papa. Of course, if Catalina had a daughter, she would never leave her in her car seat, shut inside a hot car all afternoon, the way Auntie had done to Alejandra when she was a baby. Papa was right: Catalina would never be that crazy. What Catalina really liked was that Auntie always had something fun to share, and that she was very entertaining; the opposite of Catalina, who had nothing to say since what had happened to Mama. It was as if a crumb of bread had lodged in her throat, swelling, like the cauliflower fungus that had once grown in Catalina's ear.

They finally reached the bus stop. Catalina could not believe it was happening, and neither could Papa. As they waited for the bus to arrive, he almost changed his mind and took his daughter back with him. Too many unaccompanied women, he thought. There were his daughter and Alejandra, Alejandra's older and younger sisters, an elderly housekeeper, and the neighbor-mother-aunt, supposedly in charge of the group, surrounded by bags of food, clothes, and toys. Papa's stomach clenched. He bent down, looked into her eyes, took her by the chin, and said, "You behave, okay?" Catalina nodded and threw her arms around his neck in an impulsive hug. Poor Papa. But she was so happy that she practically pushed her way onto the blue bus, which was covered with dirt and dust. The layer of dirt was so compact, Catalina observed, that in some places she couldn't see the paint even after using her fingernails. Not even when the trip got bumpy, through the poorly paved areas of the city and the rocky country roads leading them to their destination, was the dust ever dislodged.

But she didn't mind the bumpy bus. She didn't mind the windows that didn't close shut, as if to welcome the frosty mountain air and then the bittersweet aroma of the tropics. And she didn't mind the gray clouds that slowly turned purple and black, announcing a great rain as the morning came to an end and the bus descended from the mountaintop. Catalina was a perceptive child. From time to time she could smell Papa's distinctive smell, that of the little bottles hidden behind the books. But then the smell evaporated, or she forgot, and she kept playing and laughing with Alejandra, while the other passengers dozed off and Auntie began the crossword of the day in the newspaper, folded in half.

While her mother and the housekeeper were not looking, Alejandra put her head out of the window, wetting her hands and face with the veil of water that fell from a cliffside and crashed against the roof of the bus. Catalina wanted to do the same, to cool down and escape the stench of perspiration that made her dizzy. First she put her left hand out the window, then her head, but when she was about to push out her entire torso, Alejandra snitched on her. Catalina could not believe it. "Little bitch," she muttered, embarrassed and infuriated by Auntie's terrible shout in front of all the other passengers. She didn't get a chance to defend herself, to say that the idea had not been hers alone, that Alejandra had done the same thing, and that if they didn't believe her, they could look at the wet hair stuck to Alejandra's face... "Bitch," she said again, but remembered at once that the curse word ringing between her teeth was forbidden, because Mama had hated it.

She wished that a miracle could take her to Mama. A ladder, maybe, no matter how tall. She would climb up to find her... Catalina remembered the day she'd asked Mama where babies came from, and she answered, "From the sky." This had left Catalina thoughtful: "But how do they come down?" Mama had tucked her hair behind her ear and an-swered, "Down a tall, very tall ladder." Catalina had not had the courage to tell Mama that she already knew the truth, that Alejandra had told her everything, and in detail, long ago: "Babies come out of your butt, silly." Catalina knew how to hold back the urge to cry by clenching her fists. She leaned her head against the window, closed her eyes, and felt the rain come down like an African drumbeat. Soon it became a downpour and she imagined a cannibalistic dance in which she ate her friend's eyeballs, one after the other.

The inside of the bus began to get wet, and when Catalina opened the bag of sandwiches, the bus was infested with the smell of eggs. "How disgusting, you pig," Alejandra said as she watched her eat. Catalina glared at her and sent three sandwiches around. Alejandra's sisters didn't accept her offer either, but Auntie took a bite of one sandwich while trying, in vain, to cover the window with one of her plastic bags. Waves of water flooded the dusty road, the way they do in intense heat: in successive blows, first moistening the earth, then soaking it, leaving the surface soapy, and finally pooling in the ruts of the road, turning the mud into a deadly jelly. Catalina became aware of the road as a presence: a narrow, stony basilisk, hemmed in by a mountain on the right and a sheer cliff on the left. Again she smelled sweaty skin, now mixed with the eggs and the smell of the little bottles Papa had collected over the years. "Something stinks," she said, without daring to say what, thinking that maybe Papa had wanted to disappear along with the contents of the little bottles. Her words put Auntie on guard. Catalina watched her jump out of her seat like a rubber band and then walk toward the front of the bus while trying to keep her balance. It was funny to watch her because Auntie was acting like a dog, wrinkling her nose and sniffing the way dogs do in the trash, until she found what she was looking for. She didn't like it at all. She started to tremble: the man riding shotgun, unaware of Auntie behind him, was throwing a bottle of alcohol to the driver, who caught it in mid-air and drank from it openly, chugging it down. Then he shook his head and said something like "Agrrrr." Catalina knew that noise. Papa made it sometimes when he sat in the living room with the lights off. Mama had, too, as she bent over the metal basin, pulling her scarf from her head and begging, "Please leave me alone!"

Auntie, who was still on her feet and looked very worried, her face red with fury, began to yell at the driver, or rather the man riding shotgun, since the driver himself was ignoring her, swishing the alcohol around in his mouth, then swallowing. The downpour showed no signs of letting up; the bus was lurching over the road and Alejandra took Catalina's hand, without saying a word, waiting to see what her mother would do. Auntie began to scream, telling the other passengers about the alcohol, telling them the driver was going to kill them all, but nobody else said anything. Some slept, others just looked at her in silence. A voice in the back mocked her, saying, "It's no big deal, *vieja*." Alejandra's housekeeper turned toward the man and said, "Shut up, asshole." The voice in the back said, "*Maestro*, if they're that upset, let them get off the bus." Catalina took a deep breath. Mama had taught her to do that in order to calm down in difficult situations.

The bus stopped, then it backed up to make room for a truck going up the narrow, snaky road. Catalina pushed herself close to the window. The bus was very close to the edge of the cliff—so close Catalina could see the deep green valley below. Papa had told her that dying didn't hurt. Being sick hurt, but not dying; you didn't feel anything. That's why she shouldn't worry about Mama, because death was like falling asleep. Catalina leaned her head against the glass, thinking of Mama, but this time she was startled by the noise of the engine. The rear wheel of the bus lifted in the air, and the driver accelerated desperately, trying to return it to the road. The rain kept pouring down, the bus was swaying and the girls were silent, their eyes wide and expectant, while a damp, desperate Auntie began to rip off strips from the crossword, writing on them in large block letters. She sat down and gave each one of the girls a folded-up strip of newspaper. She told them not to open the note, and they each stuffed theirs in their pocket without a word, except for Catalina, who hid it between her knees, her face growing pale as she read. "If anything happens," the note said, "the driver was drunk." Catalina clenched her teeth tightly as a void opened up in her stomach and in her heart: Poor Papa. She felt these words in her chest, and began to pray.

WUTHERING

THIS MORNING I STILL felt a little angry with my grandmother, even though technically we made up last night. So I stayed away from her, to punish her, to make her feel bad about having discovered me like she did, to prove that it was actually her fault, that I was the innocent one. I hate how I'm always supposed to act as if I owe her something, to smile and smile; it's like constantly being reminded to improve my posture, when slouching is so comfortable.

To avoid her, I decided to sunbathe in the garden: something she hates, and I know why. First, she hates how dark I get. It's not about sunburn as much as the fact that it bothers her to see my skin so obviously brown. Second, she hates my bikini, so small that it barely covers me—something she can't ignore when I flop over onto my back. Mission accomplished, but just to be sure, I added a third thing she can't stand: I put my headphones on, cocooning myself with music.

The sun here is bloodthirsty. If it were a deity, it would be a sadistic one, perversely gratifying itself with the pleasure of roasting human flesh. I can feel its power soaking into my body. Meanwhile, my grandmother snips buds from the rosebush: plants, too, can get sunburn. She bustles around for a while and then stops, casting her shadow directly over my body. Even though I don't turn over, I know she's there, blocking my sun. After a while, she moves away without saying a word.

My grandmother doesn't make things easy for me. She's not like my mom: instead of exploding, she likes to dig into me sideways. It's much more creative that way...Now she drops a copy of *Wuthering Heights* on my towel, plucks away one of my headphones, and enunciates slowly, "Emily Brontë was a genius. They say she was anorexic, always fasting."

It's a low blow, after what happened last night.

"Wuthering, what does that word remind you of?" she asks.

"Not a clue," I respond, still annoyed, but in my head, words spring to mind: wuthering, blubbering, blustering. Nausea, anguish, despair.

She sits on the edge of the garden box, barely shaded by the roofline, so close to my towel that I have to turn over and look at her. From this angle, her eyes appear to glow.

"Wuthering is a powerful, sorrowful word," she says, as if nothing had ever come between us, "a scourging wind, as tragic as Emily's own life."

I allow her to make inroads into my anger. Her limpid gaze is a trap. I love words so much. She knows this. We collect them together, although we usually travel on different paths. When it comes to gay writers, for example, she goes for Verlaine, while I give myself entirely to Rimbaud and Wilde and Capote. I love gay writers; and my grandmother? She loves Baudelaire.

"Wuthering," I blurt out, "like a squall, a tempest."

She smiles benignantly. "Downpour, deluge, inclemency."

"Desolation?" I offer, feeling a little pretentious.

She looks at me, pleased. I think about something my sister likes to say: women are so "appreciative." And it's true. No matter what we get, we're appreciative…My grandmother knows that I can't resist her attentions, however small.

A lot of people don't know that *Wuthering Heights* is a book, and not just a classic film. I didn't. She disarms me.

"Emily wrote *Wuthering Heights* when she was 28. She published it under a man's name: Ellis Bell."

For a second, I think about launching into a feminist screed like the ones I hear at home, but that kind of thing would bounce right off my grandmother. So instead I ask the first thing that pops into my head: "Why?"

"Why what?" she looks at me blankly. "You mean, why did she use a pseudonym?"

I nod, tentatively.

"I think it was to avoid hurting her brother."

She explains that their father, Patrick Brontë, was an Anglican priest, an eccentric widower with six children: five girls and a boy. His son Branwell bore the brunt of his family's expectations, and he couldn't handle the pressure. He ended up passing through life without leaving a mark. Overshadowed by his sisters' talent, ravaged by opium and alcohol, he finally succumbed to tuberculosis.

"It's amazing how poisonous the expectations of those who love us can become," I comment, pleased with this oblique reference to my own situation, but she doesn't answer; her reproach is obvious.

When a conversation shuts her out, she's content to let it languish. Drama annoys her (which is partly why she annoys me).

I fill the silence. "You said there were five sisters?"

"Maria, Elizabeth, Charlotte, Emily, and Anne." She pauses briefly and closes her eyes before going on. "No one in that family was born under a lucky star. The four older girls were sent off to boarding school when Maria was eleven and Emily was only six. That's where Maria, the oldest, and Elizabeth, the second oldest, died of tuberculosis, hunger, and, without a doubt, sorrow."

"Sorrow," I repeat. The sun burns away sorrow, pricking at my legs and shoulders. Tonight the pain will make me scream, but I don't care. I close my eyes and focus on my grandmother's solemn, warm voice.

"They were killed by a teacher at the school, Miss Andrews. Andrews! Never forget an evil name," she admonishes me, and I promise to remember. To justify her rancor, she describes in detail the torments they endured.

"This Miss Andrews became obsessed with Maria. She beat her and punished her, even when she was practically on her deathbed."

I repeat it all back so that I won't forget her name. What I really want to know more about is Charlotte and Emily, those windswept girls. I get up; I need a glass of water and a hat. I bring them over.

"So why was Emily always fasting?" I ask, knowing I'm not going to like what I hear.

"Because she, unlike some, had reasons to want to die."

Although my grandmother's words hurt me, it doesn't seem to be deliberate. Or do her eyes hold a gleam of satisfaction? I resist the urge to fight back; I'd rather focus on Charlotte and Emily.

"How did they go on living?" I ask, almost to myself.

"Creating imaginary worlds together. It was their favorite game: Charlotte and Branwell invented Angria, while Emily and Anne had Gondal. They made their own tiny books with the history of each nation written in minute letters."

She tells me about the moorlands: rocky, inhospitable, exposed oceans of grass. That's where, sheltered in a little stone house, they forged an existence beyond their poverty. My grandmother describes them writing together at night, after finishing their chores, by the light of a lantern. Lantern, I think, is a wonderful word.

"Sometimes sorrow ceases to be blue, and its yellow tones make it easier to bear. It's as if, for a moment, sorrow could be beautiful," I say out loud, not expecting anything. My grandmother listens, gives me another smile, and continues with her story.

"One day, Charlotte, Emily, and their little sister Anne discovered that each of them had secretly written a novel. They decided to publish their books under the names of Currer, Ellis and Acton Bell, choosing male names to hide their identity. They never told Branwell—he was already lost to them—not even when their books became bestsellers."

I interrupt her. "They were betraying him, and they knew it!"

"I always thought they were protecting him, but maybe you're right," she says, and that small concession is a victory for me. "At any rate, it was why Branwell's death devastated them so completely. Emily, who for years had been anorexic, stopped eating entirely and refused to see a doctor. After three months, she died of tuberculosis, and five months later, so did Anne."

"Then Charlotte was the only one left?"

"Not for long. She died a month before her 39th birthday, after publishing two more novels."

Her eyes seem less liquid, deeper, more opaque. She says I can keep the book, if I want to. I thank her. She lovingly thumbs through the pages and asks me to read part of the introduction: an excerpt of a famous letter. I read it out loud: "The great trial is when evening closes and night approaches—At that hour we used to assemble in the dining-room—we used to talk—Now I sit by myself—necessarily I am silent."

"That's Charlotte?" I ask.

"Yes, that's Charlotte, alone amidst the wuthering."

The sun sits low in the west now; it no longer burns. My grandmother, or perhaps it's the golden afternoon, leaves me speechless.

SLEEPING DRAGONS

Bear this in mind about the circumstances of my story: I was a young, sad, semi-foreign girl going on a journey. Not for vacation, but for work, although I would be paid under the table, as a production assistant for a documentary. It was July, 1992. In those days I was an atheist; or maybe I should say an agnostic; or perhaps it would be closest to the truth to recognize that my heart had been broken. Consequently, on account of my bitterness, please maintain some skepticism and a deliberate attitude towards everything you will hear about my trip.

I still have no idea why they hired me, given that I had no technical expertise. To be honest, I didn't care about the documentary, much less the witchcraft or magic that everyone else seemed obsessed with. My one goal was to disappear, and if I could get paid for it, all the better. We spent a week in a 4x4, traveling first from La Paz to Ciudad de Piedra, then back to La Paz and on to Curva, the village of the Kallawaya doctors.

We left on a Sunday. There were three of us: the director, the cinematographer, and me. There was also a guide, named

Victor. When the two men announced that we were traveling with a guide, I immediately pictured a short, dark-skinned guy, but Victor was a freckled and reasonably affable redhead. He was large and superstitious, but he acted like he played on the home team, and that's what was so strange. He spoke a number of languages without putting on airs, going from Aymara to Quechua, German to English, "kicking it" over to Spanish and then to Puquina, the language of the witch doctors. I found myself irritated by his geniality, his insistence on talking to me, although not by the joints he was fond of smoking.

We set out at six in the morning, and Victor suggested that we stop in Comanche to see the famous *Puya raimondii*, the Queen of the Andes. "Ah," I said, and closed my eyes against the sun's glare. I could still hear, however, Victor's voice: "We'll be able to see the big ones, a hundred years old," he promised the director, who asked, "Is it true they can grow to be 13 feet tall?" Victor's voice rose suspiciously high: "Ohhh..." he exaggerated, "they can get up to 40 feet tall, with more than 500 flowers." Yeah right, I thought to myself. But when we got there, we didn't even have to walk around; there on a scraggly, rocky hillside, a Queen of the Andes jutted out of the ground like a skyscraper. My colleagues estimated that it was at least 30 feet tall. "It looks like a prehistoric pineapple," the director said, and I was silent. We ate and we filmed, then we went on our way toward the church of San Antonio Abad. I slept for a good while.

When I woke up, Victor was saying that God existed in these parts, that Pachamama, the Earth Mother, could produce signs, that it was a miracle the murals even still existed. We got to the village and parked in front of the church. We went in. The murals were as advertised. I shot them a quick, impious glance because I was seized by a dark nausea and had to run for the door. Searching for light, I stumbled toward the plaza and there, from a sun-warmed concrete bench, I saw an apple tree; a single apple tree with dusty leaves, hung with red fruit. If that was a supernatural sign, like Victor was saying, it definitely wasn't for me. I threw up into the planter, bracing myself on the tree trunk. Victor brought me a water bottle and sponged my forehead, rubbing the back of my neck freely, as though we were friends; and I was in no mood to say thank you. We filmed and we left.

That afternoon, we stopped in Caquiaviri; the village was quiet and the streets were deserted. Victor had a thought: "I'm an idiot!" he said, "Let's try the arena." And that's where everyone was. Minibuses and pick-ups were parked all around the rectangle of earth. There was a dance, when they brought out the bull. The matador wore sandals and waved his colorful woolen scarf as he fought the bull and tried to snatch the bundle of money tied to its neck. People shouted. The cinematographer took just a few quick shots because we judged the mixture of alcohol and dynamite to be, quite simply, flammable.

That night, on a lonely stretch of road, Victor announced that right over there was the sleeping dragon: an elusive mountain, difficult to see. The moon was full, and I swear that I could see it—the dragon—silhouetted against the sky, stretched out on the ground. Of course, I kept my mouth shut. I finally managed to fall asleep, sinking into the commotion of a destructive and superficial dream, until we got to Ciudad de Piedra. Victor told us that an Inca curse had turned the city to stone. His story was ridiculous.

We returned to La Paz and, a few days later, set out again for Curva. Victor greeted me with enthusiasm. Shaking my hand, he asked, "You dreamed about the dragon, didn't you?" I shook my head, blushing. The director wanted to drive straight through to the Ulla Ulla biosphere reserve. Victor talked non-stop, looking at me in the rear-view mirror. He had green eyes.

He said that near Charazani was Tuana, the hill that hid the city of El Dorado. He also told us that once in Curva, at a festival, a peasant from the village of Amarete got so drunk that he started dancing and throwing sticks of dynamite up in the air until his arm was ripped to shreds. Victor said that a Kallawaya doctor bandaged the man's stump with a rag full of herbs. "Years later I saw him again, with his stump healed beautifully," he told us.

The Ulla Ulla reserve had a protected area for vicuñas. "They're so photogenic," the cinematographer said. For lunch we had vicuña. "This one swallowed a rock and choked to death," they explained to us at the camp. The next day we ate vizcacha, while the rodent's head—like a long-eared chinchilla—dangled from the window. "Isn't it beautiful, too?" the cinematographer joked, noticing that I barely touched my food. Victor sat down next to me and, discreetly, pushed the bits of meat off my plate.

We decided to set out at sunrise. The 4x4 started up easily but, once we got on the road, we drove 300 feet and the motor died. The director rolled the car back and, when we got to the turnoff, the motor started up again. Victor said that to get to Curva you had to believe, you couldn't go there unless you had faith. The motor started up, we drove 300 feet, and the motor died, over and over. We changed drivers. The director gave the wheel first to Victor and then to the cinematographer, but neither of them got us any further than before.

They opened the hood to check the motor, even though it was clear that this was not a mechanical failure. I stood by the side of the road, with my hands in my pockets, for the first time on the trip, without resistance. Victor planted himself directly behind me: "The Kallawaya can heal anything, did you know that?" he whispered into my neck. His breath penetrated my body, from spine to heels. "I can go with you to find out," he said, pausing in a way that made me nervous. "But you're going to have to say please," he added. The director decided to try the road to Curva one last time, before turning around and heading back to the city. Victor said he'd drive and they sent me to the back seat. But this time it was my eyes in the rear-view mirror, while the motor started up again and our tracks disappeared behind us on the road.

A WRISTWATCH, A SOCCER BALL,
A CUP OF COFFEE

AT AGE SIX, HE learned to tell time, counting by fives: five, ten, fifteen, twenty, all the way up to sixty. He'd asked "Is it time yet?" so often that his grandfather gave him his own wristwatch, to quiet him. That precise moment brought him a gloomy awareness of the passage of time.

"It's big on you."

"Not really, Abuelo."

His grandfather fitted two fingers between the strap and the child's delicate wrist. He smiled. "Give it here, we'll add a couple of extra holes."

The boy slid the watch up from his wrist until it hugged his bicep closely, like a soccer captain's armband.

"Give it here."

The boy did. At the sound of a whistling, exhausted burst of coughing, he turned toward the wall that separated them from the next room. "Mamá?" he asked, praying for at least a temporary relief of the labored gasps that sounded almost like choking.

Abuelo placed a hand on his knee. "Did you know that the very first pilots wore their watches just like you? They used a cord to tie a pocket watch to their arm or leg."

The boy shook his head.

"Back then, planes didn't have instruments, and there was no such thing as a wristwatch. So, they made their own instruments. What do you think about that?"

"Scary," the child said, wide-eyed, hungry to hear more, trying to forget about the coughing.

"They were brave," Abuelo said. With warm authority in his voice, he went on, "Don't worry, she's okay."

"Can I wear it to school?"

"You can."

"Abuelo?"

"Hmmm?" The old man was punching a hole in the strap with his knife.

"I want to play goalie."

"But I thought you liked to kick." He lifted his eyes from the strap. "Is it because of your leg?"

"No, yes, well…" The boy looked at the ceiling. "It's because of my limp, Abuelo. They laugh at me."

"So what? The great Garrincha had polio, just like you. And he's got more than a limp—he's knock-kneed, he has a crooked spine, and to top it all off, he's really ugly." The old man chuckled loudly.

"But Abuelo, I'm not Garrincha, and I don't play for Botafogo."

"Do you like to kick or not?"

"Yes."

"Good, then. It's settled. That's the only thing that matters and if anyone laughs, you sock them. Besides, we haven't practiced this much for nothing. Or are you too scared?"

"No, Abuelo."

"That's my boy!"

The child gave him a timid, melancholy smile. In the next room, another burst of coughing made the bedsprings groan. The two of them were silent for a moment, motionless, until it was calm again.

"Abuelo," the boy spoke quietly, "is it time yet?"

"Not yet," said the old man, without glancing at the watch.

The boy picked up the pewter cup from the wood table and took a sip of coffee. The old man had taught him how to drink coffee, black coffee, when he was very small.

"Did you ever fly on a plane?"

"No."

"Will you, ever?"

"I don't know. Maybe."

"Will I?"

"I'm sure you will."

"Would you like flying?"

"I don't know," he said, fitting the watch to his wrist. "Here, let me buckle it."

"Abuelo?"

"What is it?"

"Don't go."

"Let's not start that again."

"Why can't we go with you in the truck? I promise I'll take care of Mamá and I won't fool around with my soccer ball."

"Look at that, it's a perfect fit," said the old man, ruffling the fine hair that almost covered the boy's eyes.

"I don't want you to go."

"Don't cry." His voice was stern and gentle at the same time. "You're a man now."

"That's not true, I'm only six."

Abuelo produced a white handkerchief and wiped the boy's nose.

"Why can't I go with you to the mine? Mamá could go too."

"The mine is no place for a sick woman." He tucked a bundle of folded bills into the boy's shorts pocket. "There you go, for until I come back."

"But what if she..."

"She'll be all right, she's strong. You know how to make her laugh."

Now the old man was sipping coffee from the pewter cup. The room began to grow dark as the afternoon waned: dark and cold.

"Abuelo,"—the old man's eyes were very red—"are you scared?"

"No." He sipped the cold coffee.

"I am." The boy's voice trembled. "I don't want to be left alone."

"You won't be."

"But you're old"—his voice broke—"and what if you..."

"Hush!" he ordered, "I'll be fine, I promise you."

The boy lifted his head and looked at him, very serious. He knew that nobody can promise not to die. "Will you come home soon?"

"You have my word," he said, and his eyes were as blue as the sky after a snowfall. "I'll come home soon and I'll bring you a real leather soccer ball. This one is falling apart already."

Abuelo stood up. He turned on the light and went into the other room. The boy looked at his watch. It was Sunday. After a while, the old man came out with his coat on, hat in hand. Together they walked out to the street.

"Are you going to keep kicking the ball?"

"Yes," the boy said, before the old man could finish speaking. "Like Garrincha!"

"That's right." Abuelo folded him into his arms.

The old man started the motor of the big green 1933 Volvo, maintained by the two of them with the greatest care. The boy ran after the truck, kicking his ball. He dribbled awkwardly at first and then kicked with all his might, his breath a white mist in the cold air.

Author MAGELA BAUDOIN is a journalist, writer and professor who lives in La Paz, Bolivia. Throughout her 20 years in
journalism, she has published articles, reports, interviews and
columns in different newspapers, weeklies and magazines in
Bolivia such as *La Razón*, *La Prensa* and *Nueva Crónica*. She is
the author of the novel *The Sound of H* and is the founder and
coordinator of the Creative Writing program at the Private
University of Santa Cruz.

WENDY BURK is the author of *Tree Talks: Southern Arizona*
(Delete Press) and the translator of Tedi López Mills's *Against
the Current* (Phoneme Media). She is the recipient of a 2013

National Endowment for the Arts Translation Projects Fellowship and a 2015 Artist Research and Development Grant from the Arizona Commission on the Arts. She currently works at the University of Arizona Poetry Center in Tucson where she is head Librarian.

M.J. FIÈVRE was born and educated in Port-au-Prince, Haiti, and went on to earn an MFA in Creative Writing from Florida International University. At age 19, she signed her first book contract for a Young Adult novel, and is also the author of a memoir, *A Sky the Color of Chaos: My Haitian Childhood*, published in 2014. She is secretary for Women Writers of Haitian Descent, an organization based in Florida. M.J is founder and editor of the online literary journal, Sliver of Stone Magazine, and she has published stories in English and French in several American literary journals.

ALBERTO MANGUEL is an Argentinian, Canadian, anthologist, translator, essayist, novelist and editor. In December 2015 he was made the director of the National Library of Argentina. His published works include the non-fiction works *A History of Reading* and *Curiosity*, and the novel *Stevenson Under the Palm Trees*.